"You aren't fond of deception, are you, my dear?"

Forrester's voice was low as he looked seriously into Leonora's eyes.

"You know I am not," she responded.

"But should any of your acquaintance find it necessary to play a role? Would you hold it against them?" he pressed.

"You mean yourself, don't you. Are you finally—" She darted a glance about to make certain no one was paying attention. "Are you finally going to tell me what makes you such a mystery, sir?" she queried.

"I am drawing nearer to the time when I may do so," he admitted.

"And when, sir, will that be?" she enquired.

"Ah, my dear, I would not wish to spoil the fun!"

Books by Margaret Westhaven

HARLEQUIN REGENCY ROMANCE

A CHELTENHAM COMEDY

MARGARET WESTHAVEN

Harlequin Books

TORONTO • NEW YORK • LONDON
AMSTERDAM • PARIS • SYDNEY • HAMBURG
STOCKHOLM • ATHENS • TOKYO • MILAN

To Mellyora Ashley

"...I love him, and in that word are contained birth, fame, and riches."

—John O'Keeffe
Wild Oats

Published November 1991

ISBN 0-373-31161-3

A CHELTENHAM COMEDY

CHAPTER ONE

LEONORA CLARE HAD TAKEN a seat in the quietest corner of the coffee room. This public parlour of the Plough Hotel was far from being the prowling place of dangerous young bucks and sinister roués; Leonora would wager that not one of the snuff-dusted patrons was under the age of fifty, and none of them looked likely to accost a lone young lady. Yet from habit her gloved hands were folded tightly, and her face was set in a repressive frown. At the sound of a familiar voice she looked up.

She stared, resisting the temptation to rub her eyes. Was it really Wilhelmina?

Standing in conversation with the landlord was a small, slightly plump young woman dressed in a tight cherry-red pelisse and a startling bonnet trimmed with a bunch of grapes and several feathers. The pretty, round face belonged to Wilhelmina, as did the guinea-gold curls. But the person Leonora remembered was reed-slender and slightly dowdy.

Leonora stared harder. She could be mistaken.

But the voice! It was definitely Wilhelmina's, though Leonora couldn't remember when last she had heard such a cheerful note in it.

She rose and started forward. The lady caught her eye.

"Sister!" Wilhelmina bounded across the room, scattering feathers from her shabby ostrich tippet and enveloping Leonora in a cloud of exotic scent.

The fusty gentlemen who graced the coffee room of the Plough were treated to a tearful reunion and a burst of feminine chatter. The sisters hadn't seen each other in several years.

"You look so... well, Billie," said Leonora. The word "plump" had been on the tip of her tongue, but she bit it back just in time. The opulent curves were quite becoming to her sister, but perhaps Billie didn't like the change. "Well and happy. I'm so glad you're keeping your spirits up."

Wilhelmina shrugged. She had been widowed since Leonora had last seen her. "One must go on. And you, little sister. You've grown up!"

"Don't fear hurting my feelings. I'm quite on the shelf."

"At three-and-twenty you are *not* on the shelf, dear. Take it from one many years your senior."

They chattered on, trying to bridge their separation in ten minutes. Rustling newspapers and the clearing of masculine throats eventually drew Leonora's notice. "We'd better go, Billie," she whispered. "The old man with the pipe looks fit to slit our throats. Thank you so much for coming to fetch me."

"How could I do less? I couldn't leave you to be met by the servants. Now," said Billie as the two emerged, blinking, into the bright sun of the High Street, "tell me what Papa did to you."

Leonora laughed. She looked round automatically for a coach but didn't see a likely one. All were moving, except for a gig two gentlemen were stepping into in front of the Plough. Her eye next passed over a laden barrow, which a small boy was picking up by the handles. She looked again. The luggage piled in the little cart was her own.

Billie followed her sister's glance and said casually, "I thought we'd walk home. It's such a fine morning. Now, dear, your story. What has that man done?"

"Nothing one might not have expected, I'm afraid. You must remember how Papa always was. It's simply that age and widowhood are making him more so. I've kept house for him since—well, ever since Mama died, and I'm tired of it after so many years. Tired of spending every evening in my chamber because we have objectionable guests in the house and never a respectable female. Even the vicar's lady won't visit anymore. Of late some of the men have been bringing with them, er, certain women."

"My dear!" Billie's blue eyes opened wide. "Can it have gone that far?"

"Yes. And even further. Papa has become quite close to our new cook, Billie. Mrs. Rumping retired, and the woman he hired in her place has been most complaisant. When I discovered her appropriating Mama's old room— with Papa's permission—I decided to pay you a visit." Leonora's tone was light and conversational, but it hid a multitude of worries. There was no need to mention that she had had nowhere else to go but Billie's; and it went without saying that she had had to leave home to save her own good name. Papa had gone too far. Leonora had not lived much in the world, but her mother had brought her up to know that no gently bred young lady could live in the same house with an established mistress.

"The cook! Fancy that. Papa always had his little indiscretions, but in his very own home, with his daughter in residence! He has gone beyond the line. You mustn't go back there, Leonora. We're sisters, each other's closest kin, and my home is yours from now on."

Leonora felt her eyes mist over. "Oh, Billie. How I've missed you!"

Billie squeezed Leonora's waist. "And how I've longed for your company, dearest. Only think what a dash we'll cut here. The gossips won't be able to touch me now, for what could be more respectable than having my sister with me?"

Leonora started at these words. Was Billie's own respectability in doubt? How could that be? She thought guiltily of the first impression she had had of her sister. A fast woman, she had assumed before she recognized Billie. What if she had been right?

But how to open the ticklish subject of one's own sister's reputation? Leonora couldn't imagine what to say and allowed herself to be distracted by Billie's cheerful pointing out of this assembly room and that residence of a Cheltenham notable, her attention only slightly impaired by the effects of a night spent rattling north in the stage.

"What made you come here to stay?" she asked as they followed the boy and the barrow down a winding street.

Wilhelmina smiled. "Can't you guess my reasoning? This is one of the most fashionable spas in England. It attracts its share of rich valetudinarians. I mean to marry, Leonora. And this time I will marry very well."

Leonora was taken aback. From love to money! How Billie had changed, in attitude as well as looks.

Leonora had been a child of ten when Wilhelmina, then twenty-two, had run off with the handsome but poor Captain Edward Smithers. Papa, livid at the loss of his elder child to such a middling fate, never from that day on allowed his wife or Leonora to speak Billie's name. The mother and daughter eventually found a way to keep in contact with Wilhelmina by having the errant Mrs. Smithers's letters come under cover to their vicar's wife. Once in a great while they even managed to meet with Billie before she left England.

For Wilhelmina, like many another officer's wife, found herself following the drum. Leonora sometimes envied her sister. Billie's letters from English garrison towns and later the Peninsula were determinedly cheerful, dwelling on quaint country folk and sweeping vistas rather than privation and the darker side of war. Edward Smithers advanced to the rank of major. His wife's life was a young girl's dream of romance and adventure.

Billie wrote, in short, the sorts of letters ladies caught in questionable situations generally write home to the family in order to avoid the clarion cry of "I told you so!" There was really no telling what sort of a life she lived as an army wife, for everything from military society down to the laundry was perfect once it passed by her pen.

Leonora began to sense this as the years went by. She never did have the longed-for opportunity to observe Edward and Billie together and judge if they were happy. The few times she, Billie and Mama had been able to snatch a meeting in England, Edward had been detained here or there by military business. It did seem, from Billie's new determination to marry a wealthy man, that love in a cottage—or perhaps love in a tent—had palled at some point.

"Leonora, you're dreaming."

"Oh! Sorry. What did you say?"

"I was pointing out how lucky I was to get these lodgings near the church. Quite the thing, you know, and not far from the Old Well Walk where all the visitors promenade. You can see the spire of St. Mary's from both our bedrooms. We're here!"

Leonora was a notorious daydreamer. She was able, however, to jolt herself back to the real world as quickly as she pleased. She found herself standing in front of a tall, ramshackle house of beam and plaster, one of a row of similar dwellings in what she recognized as a lower-class street. Some of the houses had To Let signs posted.

Leonora murmured something about the pleasant, large size of the house.

"I've let the second floor," Billie said with a cough. She gave directions to the lad and tripped up the steps, motioning Leonora to follow her.

Leonora hesitated. The boy was already running down the street, calling out for someone to help him carry up the heavy trunk. He disappeared into a nearby house. Did Billie really live in the same street as that dirty urchin?

"Come along, Sister," said Billie.

Leonora snapped to attention again, fighting a sense of shame. What right did she have to be critical of her sister's living arrangements?

She might have been bred in relative luxury at Greenhill, her father's Wiltshire estate, but she had never been a haughty daughter of the gentry. She had developed a touch of snobbishness and a cold public manner, true, but that was only in self-defence, a cover-up for her embarrassment at Papa's vagaries. Her pride was only a pose, she told herself often. She wasn't really a high stickler, and she wouldn't deny any worthy person her acquaintance because of a little vulgarity.

Why, then, must she feel such twinges of discomfort as Billie led her up the narrow staircase of a shabbily papered hall? Why could she find no words of admiration for the cramped sitting-room, furnished in musty plush and brocade, which she next entered?

On a table in one corner of the parlour stood a writing desk, open and crammed with papers arranged in two thick stacks. Leonora, as she passed by the desk, following Billie, couldn't avoid seeing that the top letter on one stack was a tradesman's bill; nor that the second pile was crowned with what looked to be a personal note in a spidery handwriting. A billet-doux from one of the "valetudinarians"? Surely not.

"Isn't it a cozy little place?" Billie said over her shoulder, leading Leonora through a door on one side of the parlour. "And what luck I had this spare bedroom. I've been using it to store clothes, but now it seems heaven-sent. There!" Billie's pleasant face clouded for the first time as her elegant sister entered the bare little room. "I know it's not what you're used to, dear, but—"

"Oh, Sister, it's perfect. You're an angel to have me." Leonora gave Billie a hug, cursing her own unworthy thoughts of the accommodations. "And tell me, will you allow me to help? I've hoarded my pin-money for some time, and you know Aunt Felicity left me a small annuity."

"She did?" Billie's eyes grew wide with something like envy.

Leonora nodded, a little embarrassed that she had been the favoured niece when crochety old Aunt Felicity, the most vocal denouncer of Billie's marriage aside from Papa, had made her will. "Not enough to support my own establishment. But in combination with what you have... What do you say? Shall we join forces? I brought all my money with me save what I spent on the stage, and I can soon arrange with a banker to receive next quarter's payment here."

"A widow's pension isn't much. I'd be very grateful if you could help," Billie finally said in a softer voice than Leonora had yet heard her use. "Oh, my dear, I wish I could show you off to Society here in the way you deserve. But Edward had nothing but his pay...."

Leonora wasn't surprised to hear this, and she wished she had her father in the room so she might chastise him.

Papa, in his anger at Billie's marriage, had held back her dowry. It had never occurred to him to aid his elder daughter in all the years since, though his wife and Leonora had reminded him that they did not know whether Smithers had private means. Sir John snorted at such sentimentality. Billie had made her bed, he would say in fatherly judgement, and must lie upon it.

"I'll place all I have with your bankers at once," said Leonora. She noticed for the first time that, jaunty though her sister's clothes were, they were of inferior materials. Leonora's bosom surged with guilt and anger. "And I wish I could somehow wrest your rightful portion out of Papa's hands."

Billie laughed lightly, but Leonora saw the flash of relief cross her face at the mention of funds. "Oh, as to my dowry, perhaps there's some chance Papa will approve my next marriage and relent. Can you see me received into the ancestral halls again, Leonora, with a titled husband by my side?"

"A titled husband? Can you mean someone in particular?" Leonora stared. Billie had been widowed for under a year, and it was early days to be talking of remarriage. Leonora was surprised to see her sister out of blacks, let alone deep in the waters of the husband hunt.

"There are several candidates. You'll see, dear, that your old sister can still turn a head." Billie was all smiles again, the horrid admission about finances behind her. "And wait till the bucks of Cheltenham see you, Leonora!"

Leonora protested. "Marriage isn't my first wish. Perhaps I spent too long seeing what Mama had to deal with."

"And there's your sister, throwing herself away on a penniless officer," said Billie with a nod. "Don't despair, child. There are other sorts of men in the world than Papa and—and Edward."

"Did you really throw yourself away, Billie?" asked Leonora, a little timidly.

Billie set her round jaw. "You must not ask me about it, for I don't like to dwell on it. Edward and I had our moments of happiness, but—well, he is gone now, and what is left? Money is a great sweetener, Leonora, and position as well. I shan't make the same mistake twice."

Leonora looked at her sister in concern. How unhappy *had* Smithers made his wife?

Billie rose from the bed and began to bustle about. "I'll leave you to freshen up, dear, and by the time we take off our walking things Esmé should be back from market and we shall have tea. Esmé is my maid." She hurried out, leaving Leonora to speculate on whether the staff Billie had pretended to was composed of only the one girl. Leonora's presence would create extra work. Well, she would lend her own hand to it, she resolved as she took off her bonnet and unbuttoned her redingote.

Though she longed for nothing so much as a lie-down on the narrow white bed, she didn't want to begin her reacquaintance with Billie by seeming aloof. She fluffed her blond hair in front of the smoky mirror over the chest of drawers, smoothed down her travel-creased gown, and went out into the sitting-room.

Her baggage was stacked near the front door, but there was no sign of Billie.

Leonora crossed the room and picked up a valise and a bandbox. After a moment's hesitation she picked up a second bandbox and balanced it in front of her. This box was light, packed only with her two best bonnets, but it was very tall. She had to feel her way across the room and was not surprised when she bumped into a footstool. The box which had obscured her vision pitched out of her arms.

"Bother," she muttered. She would retrieve it later.

The bandbox tumbled over the high back of a sofa which faced the cold hearth. To Leonora's astonishment, a stream of curses issued from that piece of furniture, a red-clad arm shot out, knocking her bandbox onto the floor, and a rumpled head emerged.

Leonora stared, fascinated, into a pair of red-rimmed grey eyes which might, in a less rheumy state, be attractive features of the man who possessed them. He was large, Leonora found as he stood up; he was clad in dress regimentals wrinkled beyond the point of respectability; and his thick brown hair showed more than a few streaks of silver. A bristling military moustache ornamented the ruddy face.

"A beauty, upon my word," said the soldier, his hand on his heart. He bowed.

At that moment Billie came hurrying into the room. "Leonora, this is Major Danforth. My Edward's comrade-at-arms. He was wounded during the siege of Burgos, where Edward... You mustn't mind the poor major. We were out rather late last night, and I couldn't let him walk back to his lodgings in the condition he was in." As Billie's guilty eyes slid from Leonora to Danforth, her expression changed to an accusing frown.

The major shrugged and essayed a sheepish grin at Leonora, straightening his coat.

Leonora inclined her head in Danforth's general direction, saying nothing. A jug-bitten soldier sleeping all night on her sofa! Was that Billie's idea of proper behaviour? No wonder she had been vexed by the disapproval of the gossips.

Leonora's face took on a stubborn expression. Her work was cut out for her. How lucky it was that she had come to Cheltenham!

CHAPTER TWO

LEONORA WAS HUMMING a little tune as she strolled past Hygeia House, a stone-faced manor complete with Doric colonnade. The house was the greatest ornament of Leonora's favourite part of Cheltenham. She supposed that the lanes and fields surrounding this section of the Bath Road were not even in Cheltenham proper, and that she should not walk so far from home. But she yearned so for the countryside, living in Billie's cramped lodgings.

How pleasant indeed it was to walk along the country lanes. Surrounded by fields and hedgerows, Leonora could think over her various impressions of life in Cheltenham.

In the weeks since her arrival, Leonora had kept her ears and eyes open. She suspected that Billie had curtailed her amusements upon her sister's arrival; and considering that Billie had been moving in a fast set of army people, mostly men, that was all to the good.

Billie had told Leonora that the Cheltenham Season did not start until the end of June, when Mr. King, who in the winter led the social life of Bath as Master of Ceremonies, arrived to preside over Cheltenham's summer. There would be plenty of time to introduce Leonora to Society once the more tonnish visitors arrived.

Leonora agreed. She had come to see her sister, not the Polite World at play, and she was still discovering what Billie's notion of Society might be.

What Leonora had learned so far tended to put her mind at rest. Billie was flirtatious, but so far nothing worse. She had indeed curtailed her social life upon Leonora's arrival but had been quite unequal to the task of giving up her carefully collected male admirers, the goutiest and most elderly titled gentlemen resident in the town. Luckily, annoying though these leering suitors were from a careful younger sister's point of view, they were none of them the type to whisk an unprotected widow away for a seduction in some country inn.

Billie's only wish, it seemed, was to marry one of her aged admirers and begin to enjoy the sort of frivolous and carefree life which had so far been denied her. Leonora, though she could understand her sister's feelings in a fashion, was far from certain that Billie would succeed in this project. The old gentlemen Mrs. Smithers knew were not dangerous, but neither were they entrants in the matrimonial stakes. All of them struck Leonora as the sort of aging blades who would be happy enough to pay court to a beauty so long as their peace were not cut up nor their bachelor existences threatened in any way.

One day, Leonora feared, she would be called upon to dry her sister's tears when the folly of her present course became evident.

Until that day should arrive, though, all Leonora could do was try to give sisterly advice—advice which she was afraid would not be taken, simply because she was so much younger than Billie and had no experience to speak of in Society. But happily, Billie was taking some of Leonora's hints in the matter of her behaviour. She agreed that it had not been at all the thing for Danforth to spend the night on her sofa. Danforth, in fact, had been as horrified as Leonora by the realization of what had occurred.

Leonora had found the courage to voice her surprise at seeing Billie out of mourning after less than a year of widowhood. Billie, averting her eyes, had answered that her Edward had forbidden her to put on blacks. And when the assemblies started she did not plan to dance, she added virtuously, but would attend only as Leonora's chaperon.

Leonora, while wishing that Billie's avoidance of blacks had led her to lavender and grey rather than red and bright blue, was satisfied that her sister was displaying the proper seriousness of mind. Why indeed should Wilhelmina feign grief? Clearly her marriage had been difficult for her; and Leonora's own honest nature would have baulked at a false show of sadness as much as her inherent propriety started at the absence of widow's weeds.

Those assemblies at which Billie planned not to dance would be upon them shortly, for it was early summer now and visitors were beginning to flock to the spa town. Soon there would be dances and parties aplenty, and Leonora and Billie would find themselves in the midst of all these activities.

Or would they? Leonora could not but note that, though Billie knew her share of men, she didn't number many respectable females among her acquaintance. The matrons and dowagers could be the sisters' stumbling block in any attempt to enter Society. There was no harm in Billie, but one would have to know her well to come to this conclusion, and scarcely any ladies of ton were acquainted with her.

Leonora turned down a narrow lane and climbed over a stile. Deciding not to worry until she had some reason to do so, she concentrated on the project at hand and began to scan the high banks of the lane for pimpernel. She had noticed the red flowers on her last walk in this area. Her basket was on her arm today, and she meant to gather as many of the blooms as possible. She had not been able to bathe her face in pimpernel and rainwater since leaving Wiltshire.

She was bending down to pick a handful of the flowers when someone brushed by her. A leg slightly grazed her backside, and a deep voice muttered, "Sorry, madam."

Leonora looked up and saw the broad back of a tall man: perhaps on a walking tour, she decided, from his knapsack and firm, energetic stride. He disappeared over a rise as Leonora watched.

"I accept your graceful apology, sir," she muttered, shaking her head. She rose and dusted off her gown, then ambled down the lane on the search for more pimpernel. She need not fear overtaking the man. He was walking fast enough to outdistance anyone.

"The devil!" exclaimed someone, and Leonora hurried over the rise and round a bend.

The man who had passed her a moment before was sprawled in the middle of the path. His knapsack had gone flying into a ditch. One foot was twisted under him at an odd angle.

"Oh!" Leonora hurried up and touched his shoulder. She couldn't avoid noticing as she did so that the superfine coat, though of good cut, showed signs of wear. The bottle-green fabric was shiny with hard use. "May I help you, sir? Did you step in a badger hole?"

"Did I step in a badger hole? No, madam, I find it amusing to fall flat on my face. Good Lord," grumbled that deep voice from under a felt slouch hat. Finally he pushed back the hat and glared up at Leonora. "Of course I stepped in a—oh, my."

Leonora stared into the handsome face, knowing she should cast down her lashes in response to the blatant admiration which blazed suddenly in the brown eyes. She removed her hand from his shoulder as though from a hot stove.

She was not surprised that one of the opposite sex should find her attractive. Her mirror told her that her pale blond hair and sea-coloured eyes were worthy of admiration, and the young men she had known at home in Wiltshire confirmed her honest appraisal of her looks.

What did disturb her was something which had never happened to her before: she was eyeing this stranger in the same way he was staring at her. She had never seen such a good-looking man.

He struggled to a sitting position and doffed his hat, allowing Leonora to discover that the handsome, angular face was framed by short-cropped auburn curls. He wasn't a boy. She guessed his age to be about thirty. Broad shoulders and the muscular, leather-clad legs stretched out upon the ground were testimony to athletic habits.

"Forgive my harsh words, ma'am," said the stranger. "It isn't every day I go pitching face first onto the dirt. And in front of such a charming lady! My manly pride has suffered a severe blow."

Leonora forgot as best she could that this gentleman was attractive. He was the victim of an accident. "That's as may be, sir, but the chief thing now is to make sure you haven't hurt yourself. May I help you stand up?"

He waved away the arm Leonora held out for support. Removing his right foot gingerly from the hole, he got to his feet. He dusted his boots and buckskins, then smiled at Leonora. "Couldn't be better, ma'am. Thank you for your concern."

"Walk on it," said Leonora in the severe tones of a sickroom nurse. She had put down her basket, and now she folded her arms under the bodice of her cambric gown.

With a bow he obliged. He walked two steps and lurched. "Madam." He turned back to Leonora with an apologetic smile. "I fear I'll have to beg your assistance."

"Of course." Leonora picked up her basket and his knapsack, putting the latter over her shoulder. She offered her arm and noticed that her elbow was at a level slightly below the injured man's waist. She would be of little use as a support. "Shall we go back to Cheltenham? Are you staying there?"

"Yes. Keep a look-out for a suitable walking-stick, ma'am. If I lean upon a delicate creature like you for long I'll do you an injury."

"I'm hardly a delicate creature. It's merely that you're so very large," Leonora said. He was putting scarcely any weight on her. "You may lean harder if you wish."

"Why, thank you," said the gentleman. He put one arm about her shoulders.

The familiarity startled her, but she could hardly be so missish as to withdraw her permission.

"A strange situation we find ourselves in, ma'am." The attractive brown eyes smiled down into Leonora's. "Would it be proper for us to introduce ourselves?"

"I don't see why not. I am Miss Clare." Leonora tried to keep a casual lilt in her voice, although the strong arm encircling her was no aid to her composure.

"Miss Clare, your most obedient. I am Richard Forrester."

"A pleasure, Mr. Forrester." Had he really squeezed her shoulders? Surely not. Leonora, confused, searched the lane as though she expected a walking-stick to be growing out of the grassy verge. "We should sit you down on the stile when we come to it, sir, and I'll look in the trees for a stick of some kind. We can't go all the way back to town like this."

"What a pity," said Forrester. Leonora looked up at him in indignation, and he winked.

"Mr. Forrester..."

"Your pardon, Miss Clare. I'm taking advantage of your chivalrous nature, but put yourself in my place. How often do I have the chance to wrap my arm about a beautiful young woman?"

"Quite often, I expect. Are you always so bold, sir?"

"Of course." They were only a yard from the stile now, and Forrester removed his arm from Leonora, hopped over to it and sat down. He grinned at her. "My dear Miss Clare, the world may be full of opportunities, but would you have me waste such a charming one?"

Leonora smiled against her better judgement. If not for his injury, this would be a most improper encounter. However, he *was* hurt, and if a group of the haughtiest dowagers in Cheltenham should come upon this tête-à-tête they would have no reason to censure Leonora. This reasoning made her reluctant to take Forrester to task; best, in any case, to forget his provocative words. "Sir, I'm going to look about for a walking-stick. I shall return as soon as I can. You'd better stay here and rest."

Forrester frowned. "You won't stay to flirt? My loss. Well, Miss Clare, don't go too far, and remember I'm only a scream away if you should run into trouble. Why are you out alone, by the way?"

Leonora shrugged. "I'm beyond the age to be dogged everywhere by a chaperon, and I live quietly with my sister. She doesn't have a servant to spare to trail my every step."

"Oh. Why didn't I notice your ancientness before? Now that I look closely I can tell you're all of ... fifteen."

Leonora knew he was roasting her. Furthermore, she was still young enough to be annoyed, not flattered, by such allusions. "If you're fishing for my age, sir, I'm three-and-twenty."

"I must believe a lady." Leonora was certain his slight bow was teasing. He was so good-humoured that she could not take offence. "As to the proprieties, I'm only a visitor here," he continued, "and I give way to your judgement as a native of this place."

That was more fishing, Leonora suspected. She saw no reason not to reward his curiosity a very little; he looked respectable as well as handsome, and his manner of speech was certainly that of a gentleman. She wouldn't tell him where she lived, of course, but she had no hesitation in saying, "I'm a visitor, too, as it happens. My sister and I are here for the Season. I don't know the town well as yet, but I haven't ever been reproved for walking out on my gathering expeditions on my own."

"Ah, yes, your basket. What do you gather?"

Leonora shrugged. "Various things. At home I considered myself quite the amateur apothecary; I was the only one available to care for my father's tenants. Even here, where there are no tenants, I sometimes wish to make up some potion or other. It amuses me." Somehow, she didn't like to admit that the flowers she had been gathering today were only for a beauty treatment, not something important.

"A doctor! Fancy that."

A doctor, indeed! As a woman, Leonora knew she must confine her interest in things medicinal to writing down all the remedies she could in her household book, and sometimes this limitation irked her. She was about to admit this when it occurred to her to wonder why she had confided so much to a stranger. She made haste to turn the subject.

"And you, Mr. Forrester. What brings you to this place?"

"My health. I'm taking the waters," was his instant answer.

Leonora frowned. Health? Except for his ankle, which had been in perfect order a half hour before, Mr. Forrester looked to be in bursting health. Strong shoulders, a bronzed complexion, and an energetic manner were not qualities one associated with invalids. "A—a war wound, perhaps?" she ventured.

"War? Oh, no. Merely my old trouble acting up again."

Leonora's curiosity was piqued, but she knew it would be unspeakably rude to ask what that trouble was. She made a sympathetic murmur and disappeared into the little cluster of trees to one side of the lane. She knew Forrester followed her retreating figure with his eyes. She could feel them boring into her back and minded how she walked, trying to make her gait elegant, of course, not twitching her hips about as Billie was wont to do.

She was back in a few moments carrying a straight, fallen branch for Forrester's consideration. Taking out a pocket-knife, he whittled the branch into an acceptable if rustic walking cane while Leonora watched.

"Now, sir, if you can walk with that, I'd better say goodbye."

"What? You'd leave me to my fate in this wilderness? Dashed unkind of you, ma'am. How am I to find you again?"

Leonora paused in the act of arranging her basket on her arm. "Find me again?" she asked casually.

His smile was merry as he said, "My dear Miss Clare, this rousing adventure has bound us together in a way. Haven't you heard the old Chinese proverb which says that if you save someone's life, you are responsible for him? Don't tell me you're going to fall down in your duty already."

Leonora laughed, grateful that she had no tendency to blush. "I hardly saved your life, sir."

"How do you know I wouldn't have lain there for months, nibbled by rabbits or perhaps by that badger whose house I trespassed in? You do yourself too little credit, ma'am."

"Well, consider me your saviour if you like. But I really must go; my sister will be worrying." And, after dropping a small curtsy, Leonora climbed over the stile. "Oh!" She turned back once she was safely on the other side. "Do you need help, Mr. Forrester? I don't know how you'll manage the stile with your twisted ankle."

"Don't worry. I plan to sit here for a time and absorb the beauties of nature; then I'll climb under the fence. Are you sure you must go?"

"Yes."

Forrester held out his hand. "My thanks again, ma'am. I hope to see you soon."

"Well." Leonora cast down her eyes in confusion as she put her hand in his. This would be the moment to tell him her street or at least her sister's name, if she ever did want to see him again. She wasn't bold enough. "Goodbye, then, Mr. Forrester." She hurried away down the lane.

Forrester looked after her until she disappeared beyond a turning. "Not quite goodbye, Miss Clare," he murmured.

He sat still for some time, surveying the bright day through smiling eyes. Then he proceeded to climb lithely over the stile and walk back towards the town with a jaunty step, swinging his walking-stick from one arm.

CHAPTER THREE

"A MR. RICHARD FORRESTER," said Billie in tones of deep disappointment. "A *Mr.* Forrester. Oh, Leonora." She sighed and clapped her cup of tepid tea down onto the table. "Esmé! A fresh pot."

Esmé, the pretty, dark-eyed maid-of-all-work Billie had brought back with her from Spain, flounced about clearing the remnants of the ladies' Spartan supper. Leonora didn't answer her sister until the maid had gone out of the room. Despite Billie's assertions that Esmé understood very little English, Leonora knew that the girl had a command of the language.

"Really, Billie. You never used to demand a title before you'd say how-do-you-do to a gentleman," she said as the door snapped shut behind the maid.

"I've grown wiser. Leonora, how would I feel if your living with me only resulted in your marriage to a *Mr.* Somebody? A mister whom you admit wore a shabby coat."

"I only met him; I didn't marry him. Good heavens," Leonora muttered.

"You said he was handsome. It's true we haven't spent much time together in late years, but I never remember you writing about any gentleman and calling him handsome. This horrid Forrester person has captivated you, and soon you'll be running off in the dark of night as I did, and..."

Leonora shook her head as the ranting continued. The truth was, a rout was being given tonight, at the house of the daughter of one of Billie's admirers, and Mrs. Smithers had not been invited. Leonora had brought up the meeting with Forrester thinking to distract her sister.

She had not, however, thought to overset her. Billie might well have sensed her sister's real attraction to the gentleman, but the situation was hardly desperate.

"Billie, I know. I know." Leonora reached across the table to pat her hand. "I promise not to run off in the dark of night with anyone. Mama always said I was the prudent one, and Papa's new name for me is his 'starched-up inquisitor.'"

The sisters laughed at the mention of their father, but their discussion of Sir John shortly became more serious. Leonora, to Billie's distress, hadn't escaped her home in secrecy, which Billie considered would have been much more sensible and have saved them a thousand worries about the volatile Sir John's next move.

Leonora, however, conducted her life along simple lines, scorning subterfuge of any kind. She had ordered up the gig one morning when Sir John and the cook were still abed, and had had a groom drive her out the gates of Greenhill and to the stage stop. She had even left a note for Papa, outlining her reasons for leaving and giving Wilhelmina's direction in Cheltenham.

The sight of his recent letter, in the familiar, bold fist, had shocked Billie a great deal, for she hadn't seen her father's writing in thirteen years.

The missive was a typical communication for Sir John: it threatened unspecified dramatics and ordered Leonora home. She had answered it in daughterly mildness, stating that she would never set foot on the property until her father had removed his mistress from her mother's room.

She had reached her majority and thanks to Aunt Felicity could finance her refuge with Billie indefinitely.

Leonora did feel Papa would relent someday. Perhaps when he tired of the cook he would miss Leonora's perfect running of the household. But for the present she suspected she and her father were at an impasse.

"Look upon it in this way, Billie," she said with a twinkle. "Papa may disinherit me for visiting you, and then Mr. Forrester will seem a good enough catch."

Billie replied, as she patted Leonora's hand, "Your face is your fortune, my dear. You won't throw yourself away. I know that."

She looked so determined that Leonora felt uneasy.

THE NEXT DAY WAS SUNDAY. The sisters, attired in their finest and followed by Esmé, made their way down their winding street and across the sun-dappled green to St. Mary's. Leonora was coming to love the ancient church with its one soaring spire, and as she looked up at it she felt lucky to be here in Cheltenham rather than immured at home. She had never visited a public place before, and Cheltenham was becoming a very public place. The town was fast filling for its Season. Leonora noticed, with a little pang, that her best hat and pelisse didn't look half so fashionable this Sunday as they had only the week before.

"Ladies!" called a robust voice.

Major Danforth limped only slightly as he strode towards them. He executed his best bow to Wilhelmina, followed this by one even lower in Leonora's direction, and asked if he might escort them to divine service.

"Heavens, Danforth, why so formal?" said Billie. When she saw the major's eyes slide guiltily to Leonora, she clapped her hand over her mouth to hide a giggle.

Leonora smiled her acquiescence, making up her mind to take Major Danforth aside soon and inform him once and for all that she was no longer offended by the circumstances of their first meeting. Danforth hadn't been able to look Leonora in the eye once during their acquaintance. Worse, every now and then he would stammer out some apology for his inexcusable behaviour, turning the subject before Leonora could assure him that the incident was forgotten.

"My poor major must be deep in your toils to act like such a cake, Leonora. But *he* won't do. He has nothing but his pay," Billie whispered into Leonora's bonnet.

Leonora frowned. Billie couldn't be widgeon enough to think Danforth was in love with anyone but herself. What Leonora had learned so far about the major inclined her much in his favour. Invalided out in the siege at which Smithers had met his end, Danforth had been in a position to escort Billie back to England. Leonora gathered that wherever Billie had gone in the last winter and spring, the major had gone, too. Neither one had to acknowledge their travels were related, and their almost constant proximity seemed disinterested and logical. The Cheltenham waters, for instance, were exactly what Major Danforth's doctor had advised for him, though anyone who knew the major could see that seabathing at bustling Brighton would be much more in character for a military man of his vigorous nature.

The major, in short, loved in patience, and with no hope of a return that Leonora could discern. It pained her to watch the way his eyes rested on Billie with a tenderness that couldn't be explained by mere friendship. Billie simply refused to see this. Nor could she understand, as did Leonora, that Danforth's continued embarrassment at being discovered on Billie's sofa arose, not from an infatuation with Leonora, but from shame at having disgraced himself before the widow's closest relation. Leonora was beginning to think that her sister was quite thickheaded.

The party proceeded into the church. Leonora, still preoccupied with her thoughts of Billie and Danforth, looked about at the crowd with a casual interest. Then she nearly dropped her prayer book.

Sitting not two rows ahead of her was Forrester. She had cherished hopes of seeing him again but had never dreamed it would be so soon.

She tugged at her sister's sleeve. "Do you see the tall man in the dark blue coat, sitting next to the man in brown?" she whispered. "That's Mr. Forrester."

Billie peered at the gentleman's sturdy back, then turned to Danforth, who sat on her other side. "Major, do you know anything about that man? Blue coat and reddish hair." Service had not yet begun, and now was the time to collect information.

Danforth looked. "Can't say that I do, my dear Wilhelmina."

"Well, find out," whispered Billie.

"At your service, dear lady."

Leonora was embarrassed, but at the same time she felt a little stab of satisfaction that Danforth had been ordered to find out about Forrester. She would enjoy learning more about the man she had "rescued" the day before.

After service, Leonora and her two companions walked about the lawn in front of the church. Billie greeted several older ladies with a deference which Leonora recognized as the worst sort of toadeating. Another step in the plan to marry a title, no doubt, was to curry favour with the females of the district.

Leonora only wished Billie had put her scheming in the proper order and had won the ladies' approval first. Perhaps the years of living in army circles had contributed to a lack of finesse in these matters. Army people had to live for the moment, did they not? And that might give rise to less than genteel ways. It did seem that Billie's good breeding might have gone the way of her taste in dress. Leonora writhed at each new introduction and put on a coldness which, had she but known it, did much to raise her—and by extension, Billie—in the eyes of all.

"Miss Clare," said someone at Leonora's elbow, and she looked up into the twinkling eyes of Richard Forrester. He was smiling in a peculiar, intimate way which pleased even as it disturbed. "I told you we'd meet again. And now for the proper thing. I say, Danforth." He turned to the major, who stood beside a suddenly glaring Billie. "You will present your old friend Forrester to these charming ladies, won't you?"

"Danforth," said Billie severely, "I thought you said you weren't acquainted with this gentleman."

"Made a mistake. Forrester. To be sure," said the major with a cough. Leonora thought his naturally ruddy cheeks took on a deeper glow. "Mrs. Smithers, Miss Clare . . . my old friend. Forrester, did you say it was? Ah, yes, Forrester."

Mr. Forrester bowed over the lace mitten of Mrs. Smithers, whose greeting of him was as cold and repressive as it had been fawning when she spoke to the fashionable matrons. Then he turned to Leonora and solemnly took her hand.

"This lady and I are already acquainted. She saved me, you know, Danforth." As he spoke, he was looking deeply into Leonora's eyes. Only a glint of humour in his own saved his behaviour from being objectionable.

"That so?" said the major.

"My sister told me about the incident," Billie said with an off-putting sniff. "Nothing to signify."

"I disagree, ma'am." Forrester turned to the widow. "Your sister is that rarest of creatures, the true Good Samaritan. In her charity she stopped to aid me, though I could have been the most desperate character to stalk the country since—"

"You need not remind me, sir, that my sister took a foolish chance," snapped Billie. "And while we're on the subject, what exactly *are* you if not a desperate character?"

Forrester grinned at her, then turned back to Leonora. "A careful guardian. What more could a young lady desire in a chaperon? Has anyone ever told you, Miss Clare, that your eyes are as green as the sea? Or would that be as blue? What colour *are* your eyes, Miss Clare?"

"Mr. Forrester!" said Billie. "Your boldness is extraordinary on such short acquaintance. Leonora is too shy to protest, but I must. I'm waiting for you to answer me."

"Ah!" Forrester's eyes didn't leave Leonora's. "I'd hoped to learn your Christian name. Leonora."

"Miss Clare to you," said Leonora, intercepting Billie's horrified look. She wished, for one wistful moment, that she and Forrester could be alone to continue this conversation. He was joking with her, yet she could swear there was true admiration in his manner as well as a mischievous desire to drive Billie into the fidgets.

"May I join you in taking the ladies home, Danforth?" asked Forrester, turning his ingratiating grin on his friend.

"Er..." The major hesitated, torn between Forrester's humorous but commanding look and Billie's frown.

"No, you may not, sir. Do go away, and take Major Danforth with you," said Billie. "We have my maid." She made a movement of her head in the direction of the hovering Esmé.

"Mrs. Smithers, I am your most obedient," said Forrester in the same smooth, social voice he might have used had she not just warned him off. Leonora was rendered speechless by her sister's rudeness, and Danforth's eyes were nearly popping. Leonora supposed the major had never seen his adored Wilhelmina act the protective dragon. With one last surprised glance at Billie, Danforth walked away with Forrester.

"Humph," said Billie. "What an encroaching young man. Never you mind, I'll get it out of Danforth. We'll know that fellow's income, if he has one, before the week's out. You notice he ignored my questions about who he is. Looks like a Captain Sharp to me, and a rake into the bargain. 'What colour are your eyes,' indeed. I hope you weren't taken in, Leonora. Oh! There's Lady Markham and her brother-in-law. Let's walk over that way. I even think I see her delightful stepson with her. I'm so pleased you suggested this dark blue hat for me, Sister. Lady Markham is rather a stickler in matters of dress."

Leonora allowed herself to be led away, trying not to show her boredom at being forced on another icy dowager. This Lady Markham, one glance told her, was more haughty-looking than any of the other women she had met that morning.

And the gentlemen the dowager had with her! One was a small, pale young man who looked like a grub—was he supposed to be delightful?—and the other a taller, more personable middle-aged gentleman whom Leonora recognized as exactly the raffish sort her father was forever inviting to the house. Billie must indeed be desperate to grovel before such people.

Leonora looked wistfully over her shoulder at the re-treating major and his tall companion. Forrester was not limping at all as he talked to Danforth in an earnest fash-ion. It seemed that his severely injured ankle had under-gone a miraculous cure.

She knew she ought to disapprove of such a deception, but she could not but be flattered. Had he really feigned injury to be with her? Someday perhaps she would ask him.

CHAPTER FOUR

AT LADY MARKHAM'S ELEGANT house in the Royal Crescent resided Wilhelmina Smithers's brightest hopes for the future. The widow had looked about her at the crop of Cheltenham bachelors and decided that no one would be more convenient to her matrimonial purposes than Lady Markham's brother-in-law, the present baronet.

The worthy Sir Hector was not old, and Billie had been afraid she might have to settle for great age in her quest for riches. Besides the delightful qualification of middle age, the baronet possessed an entailed estate in the country and perhaps a house in London—Billie's information was not yet complete concerning the latter detail. The Cheltenham house belonged to Lady Markham, which was a shame. But the easygoing Sir Hector had not let circumstances embitter him, though rumour had it that Elizabeth, Lady Markham had married for the Markham fortune and had succeeded by her arts in having the will altered in her favour. Sir Hector was content to lend his ton to her household, and cheerfully allowed her to feed and house him.

Billie hoped her favourite's frugality in the matter of living arrangements was not motivated by need. She did not intend to throw her handkerchief down until her findings on Sir Hector Markham were complete. A second imprudent marriage was not in her plans.

Here, then, was one reason why Billie longed to ingratiate herself with Lady Markham. Since Leonora had come to live with her, she had discovered another.

Lady Markham had a stepson by her first marriage, also living with her in Cheltenham for the Season. The young man was dullish, undistinguished; Billie couldn't remember what he looked like from one encounter to the next. But he did have one attribute which made him irresistible as a suitor.

The stepson happened to be the new holder of an ancient title: only a barony, but a respected one. Lord Stone reigned over a showplace of an estate deep in the Cotswolds. His ancestors had fought beside the Conqueror—or was it against him? Either way, no family in England was richer in history or in merit than the Barons Stone. The matchmaking mamas of the spa town were correspondingly eager to make the young baron the property of some one of their daughters.

Billie could see no reason why Leonora, with her regal manner and pale beauty, should not walk off with the catch of the Cheltenham Season. That this prize should be in the unattractive wrappings of a middling young man was a detail not to be noted.

Billie began to muse over the possibility of a double wedding, step-uncle and sister, nephew and sister. What a close-knit little family they would be!

The only dropped stitch was the sad fact that an obscure, widowed Mrs. Smithers living on the fringes of Society hadn't been able to storm the ramparts of the Markham house in the Royal Crescent. She could hardly take steps towards Leonora's future until she was received there. Billie had, however, already batted her eyes at Sir Hector to enough effect that he attended her own little soirées.

One morning Billie went out to pay a call upon Mrs. Pickering, the widow of Smithers's general, a lady who received Mrs. Smithers out of sentiment for the regiment and for no other reason. Billie, though aware of this, waited upon her regularly, for she understood she must take whatever foothold she could manage in the cliff-face of respectable Society. And she had also come to comprehend, partly through Leonora's lectures, partly through her own experience, that she would have to conquer respectable Society if she were to make the rich marriage she had set her sights upon.

Leonora wouldn't join her sister in the outing. She had paid one such call, the week of her arrival in Cheltenham, and she had hated the disdain apparent in Mrs. Pickering's manner. Leonora didn't scold Billie for toad-eating nor cite her own distaste as a reason for staying in. She offered as her excuse that she meant to brew a new kind of skin ointment. Billie couldn't argue while she continued to benefit from her sister's clever concoctions, but she was disappointed. "Mrs. Smithers and Miss Clare" sounded so much more genteel on the lips of a starchy butler than did plain "Mrs. Smithers."

For her visit Billie wore a mouse-coloured pelisse borrowed from Leonora. Only the garment's extremely tight fit and excessive length, the sisters not being of a size, spoiled the effect of elegance the widow was striving for. Billie didn't notice this and exulted in her quiet appearance.

Once safely past the portals of Mrs. Pickering's house in St. George's Place, Billie sipped tea and murmured about the latest arrivals, reminding herself as she nibbled at too many biscuits that she had been born a Clare and was quite good enough to chat with the likes of Lady Whitton and Mrs. Harborough. The ladies were even beginning to warm to her, asking questions about Leonora, whom Billie didn't hesitate to claim she was chaperoning for the summer Season.

That one of Leonora's elegance and reserve should put herself under the wing of Mrs. Smithers was a recommendation in itself. Billie relaxed a little, satisfied that her social status was on the rise.

"Lady Markham." The ringing voice of Mrs. Pickering's butler broke into the cloud of gossip and refinement. An imposing female paused on the threshold of the drawing-room.

Billie nearly clasped her hands at this stroke of luck. Her eyes gleamed with an avid expression she rarely directed towards members of the female sex.

Lady Markham was a tall woman, whose ample bosom and Roman profile gave her a regal air. Her iron-grey eyes swept the room carelessly before she advanced to her hostess and took the best seat in the room, which had been left vacant as if by design. Lady Markham, though she deplored flashy dress in others, was noted for her imaginative headgear. Today she had on a concoction involving lovebirds, sprigs of wheat, and various fruits. Every female in the room stared at the chapeau in evident fascination.

Her ladyship had organized sundry fêtes and gaieties in past Seasons. She rivaled Mr. King, the Master of Ceremonies, in her zeal to see Cheltenham amused. Thus no one in the room, with the exception of Billie, who was a comparative stranger, was surprised to hear the lady open at once the subject of the boring present Season and her plan to enliven it.

"I've run into a snag in the production," she confided, accepting tea and cakes from her hostess. "My little heroine has turned missish on me and won't perform."

"Miss Derwent has cried off?" someone asked.

Mrs. Harborough whispered into the puzzled Billie's ear that Lady Markham had been organizing private theatricals.

"Theatricals. Fancy that," Billie murmured back, unable to connect such a frivolous pastime with someone of Lady Markham's evident distinction.

"The chit gave her health as an excuse," Lady Markham was saying. "Can't insist, can I? A shame, I call it, with the rest of the cast all set to go. Lord Stone is the hero, you know."

Billie's cup clattered into its saucer as an idea struck her.

"My dear Lady Markham." She spoke up with a gracious smile. "My sister, Leonora Clare, is staying with me. She adores theatricals, and she's very talented. She'd be charmed to offer her services."

"How kind of you, Mrs. Smithers," cried someone.

Many sly glances went Lady Markham's way. The grande dame peered over her quizzing glass at the army widow. Lady Markham had never spoken two words to Mrs. Smithers, though she remembered the brash blonde. Hadn't this particular bold piece been casting sheep's eyes at brother Hector? Only the other day at church, Lady Markham had been disgusted anew by the widow's flirtatious behaviour. Her sister, though: would that be the quiet, well-bred creature who had seemed properly embarrassed by Mrs. Smithers's antics?

Lady Markham looked about her and seemed to sense that such a generous offer as Mrs. Smithers's couldn't be rejected out of hand in the august company of tattlemongers. "I believe I met your sister after service on Sunday," she said, still eyeing Billie narrowly.

Billie swallowed her indignation—for she did have some pride left—and answered, "You did indeed." She under-

stood that this was Lady Markham's way of ascertaining
Leonora's identity.

One of the other ladies remarked the tension and broke
in with a compliment on Leonora's beauty and quiet manner. "Such a delicate-looking and elegant creature. Fancy
her being an enthusiast for theatricals!"

Billie managed to return a pleasant nod.

"I'd be delighted to accept your sister's services, Mrs.
Smithers," said Lady Markham, with the air of royalty
bestowing a boon. She fished in her massive reticule and
came up with a thick sheaf of papers bound in cloth. "My
own copy of the play. Do take it to your sister. I'll send a
note round about rehearsals."

Billie accepted the papers with a curtsy and went back
to her chair, where she leafed through the pages. "*Wild
Oats,* a Comedy by John O'Keeffe," the title page proclaimed. The play was copied out in a fine hand. Billie
frowned in surprise. She had never heard of a playwright
called O'Keeffe. Somehow she had imagined the dignified
Lady Markham would choose a Shakespearean tragedy.
She had already envisioned Leonora in the role of Juliet or
Ophelia.

Lady Markham, still watching the widow with the attention a cat might give to an insect, saw the puzzled look.
"A light comedy, Mrs. Smithers. Precisely the thing for the
amusement of my guests. There is too much tragedy these
days, don't you agree? The war and all. And I'm told the
Theatre Royal will be doing several tragic pieces this summer. I mean this to be a private, select entertainment. To
cheer us." She dabbed at one dry eye with an embroi-
dered scrap of linen. "I still feel the loss of my elder stepson." Captain Richard Manders, the last Lord Stone, had
died at Badajoz a mere year before; Lady Markham and
her family had but recently come out of mourning.

"Who would have thought the younger boy would inherit the Stone estates and title?" she went on. "But God disposes. Yes, we need a light play, a comedy, to see us through these tragic times. Your sister will be a Quakeress, Mrs. Smithers. No need to worry for her dignity. She plays the heiress of an estate who wants to share her wealth with all her neighbours."

"Heavens," said Billie, eyes wide. She bent her head to the play, trying to hide her agitation. The commitment made, she was beginning to be apprehensive over Leonora's reaction.

Lady Markham held forth on the great theatrical traditions of the town of Cheltenham. "I was visiting here, many years ago, when I was privileged to see Mrs. Siddons perform in the role of Belvidera. *Venice Preserv'd*, you know, by Otway. An old-fashioned play, but a charming one. There was no proper theatre then. The players made do with a fitted-up malt house out in the wilds where that Mr. Pitt is thinking of building his new developments. I had thought of taking *Venice Preserv'd* as our project, but it is a tragedy, alas. My dear stepson Lord Stone has no desire to play a tragic hero, glorious though he would be in almost any role. Jack Rover in *Wild Oats* will exactly suit his wishes."

The ladies variously nodded and murmured. Billie, for one, was certain that that forgettable boy, Lord Stone, wouldn't shine in the part of a Shakespearean hero or any tragic ranter. Would he be even passable as this Rover, she was wondering as she flipped through the pages looking for scenes Leonora and Stone would play together.

She barely heard Mrs. Harborough say to Lady Whitton that Mrs. Siddons was a delightful creature, such a perfect lady. Mrs. Harborough knew the great actress and her family. They could hardly be considered typical theatrical people . . . they were intimate with the Duchess of York.

Billie's ears pricked up at this tidbit. Fancy a theatre family knowing His Majesty's daughter-in-law! If professional actors rose to such heights, not even Leonora could pretend that amateur theatricals were unrefined.

LEONORA, WITH THE SULLEN aid of Esmé, had had a busy morning brewing and bottling. She had not only a new hand cream, but a vegetable rouge which she hoped would be more subtle than the Spanish papers Billie sometimes used. She was taking off her apron in the sitting room when there came a knock at the door.

She went to answer it. Esmé was still in the cellar storing away the cosmetic implementia, and Leonora did not like to cower behind a closed door. The visitor would be some one of Billie's gallants. With any luck it would not be Lord Eldon, for Leonora had promised that gouty gentleman a special dry poultice which she hadn't got round to making.

Major Danforth stood at attention, his hat in his hand. "Miss Clare," he said in the direction of the carpet.

"Come in, sir," said Leonora pleasantly. "I think it's time we had a little talk."

The large military man met her eyes for an instant. His expression flashed out alarm, then changed to grim determination. His limp pronounced as it always was after a climb up two flights of stairs, he accepted a seat on a hard chair.

"I don't wonder you're still angry at me, ma'am," he began. "To find me snoring away on Mrs. Smithers's sofa must have shocked you very much. There was nothing in it, I assure you—"

"Major Danforth," said Leonora. "Do not mention it. Let us forget about that incident once and for all. I'm quite pleased that you haven't been so very, er, inebriated in the whole time of our acquaintance as you must have been on that unhappy occasion."

Major Danforth sighed, wiping his forehead with a large pocket handkerchief. "An unfortunate lapse and a rare one, madam, I assure you."

"I wager my sister drove you to it, poor man, with the offhand way she treats you," mused Leonora.

Danforth stared. "By George, Miss Clare, you've guessed it. That woman is driving me into Bedlam."

Leonora laughed. "I didn't really have to guess, for I can tell you've a tenderness for her. I hope my sister will get over her absurd ideas on wealth and position before she loses you."

"There's little danger of her losing me," said Danforth gruffly.

Smiling, Leonora said, "I'm so glad, sir. You seem right for her, and someday she will come to realize it. And don't think you have any serious rivals. Billie doesn't know how to get into Society. I say thank heaven she hasn't insinuated herself into the good graces of any of those old harpies she fawns over. That Lady Markham, for instance! I cannot like her. Looking down her nose at *us*. We're a baronet's daughters, and she is only the widow of one. Oh, and also of a baron, but I haven't heard her touting her own antecedents."

"You find the starched-up harridans wherever you go, Miss Clare. Can't be helped."

"I know." Leonora paused. "I used to regret, when I was stuck out in the country with Papa, that I wasn't able to go more into Society. But if Society is nothing but a clutch of high-nosed old ladies . . ."

"Oh, it ain't that, ma'am. Give the Season here a chance. A pretty girl like you, bound to find admirers." Danforth gave her a look that was very near to a wink, involving a quirked eyebrow and a sly expression. "You've already found at least one."

Leonora looked away. He must be referring to Forrester. Turning her eyes to Danforth again, she said, "Tell me, sir, since we're being direct, are you an old friend of Mr. Richard Forrester's, as he claims, or did he only presume upon a slight acquaintance with you the other day at church?"

There was an ominous pause while the major appeared to think furiously. "We're acquainted," he finally said.

"From the army, perhaps?" asked Leonora, her suspicions growing that Mr. Forrester was in some way not what he seemed.

"Army? No, ma'am!" Danforth denied this idea quickly. "You see, your sister didn't know him, did she? I couldn't have met him in the army. Must have been somewhere else."

"Must have been? Don't you know?"

The major put a hand on his chin and fondled his moustache. "School. Must have been at school."

Leonora looked suspicious.

"Well, known Forrester for years, ain't I?" the major said, as though in self-defence. "A fellow's bound to forget that sort of detail. School it was."

About to raise the question of which school, and why in that case Danforth and Forrester seemed to be of such disparate ages, Leonora realized what an undue interest in Forrester her interrogation betrayed. She might indeed have such an interest, but she shouldn't expose herself.

"Isn't it nice to meet an old friend," she said instead. "I warn you, sir, my sister will be bombarding you with questions about Mr. Forrester's income and ancestry. She's taken it into her head that he's a danger to me." She laughed. "But enough about that gentleman. Tell me instead something I've longed to know, sir. How did you meet my sister?"

The major's eyes lit up, and he launched into an involved tale of a hillside near a garrison town and a lovely golden-haired lady in white. "First words out of her mouth were, she was married to Smithers. Dashed bad luck. Did the only thing I could do. Scraped acquaintance with Smithers so as to get invited to their place and become her friend. And to be of service if the lady had need. Couldn't call on a stranger, could she, but nothing more natural than getting help from a friend of her husband. Glad I had at least that right when poor Smithers's time came and she needed me at last." He sighed. "Had to thank heaven for my own wound, for had I not been invalided home I would have lost her."

Leonora's eyes nearly misted over at the recital of such disinterested gallantry; and she was newly vexed with Billie for treating this devoted soul much as she might a courier or a footman. "My sister never talks much about Edward. Were they happy?"

A furtive expression played on the major's rough countenance. He began to mutter some commonplace remarks. Then he gave a snort, looked Leonora full in the eye, and said, "I'm prejudiced, ma'am, there's no denying that, but deuce take it, she's bloomed since he died. He—he confided to me once, while we was in our cups, ma'am, that he'd been disappointed. Misunderstood about her portion. The girl was twenty-two, and he'd figured her money was in her own hands, so to speak. They had to run off, but Smithers hadn't thought that your father, ma'am, could hold back the dowry."

"Oh!" Leonora was aghast at this revelation. "My poor sister. And I suppose he was cruel to her?"

"Don't think so, ma'am. They weren't too friendly with each other after the first, ah, bloom of romance passed by, but I don't think there's more to it."

Leonora was reminiscing. "When I saw her the day I arrived I hardly recognized her. She was no longer slender and pale, and I noticed at once how becoming the change was to her."

"Out from under Smithers's thumb," was the major's theory. "Never looked better, did she? Can't tell you what it did for her, that particular cannonball."

Leonora drew in her breath. She hadn't heard anything about her deceased brother-in-law which inclined her in his favour; still, she wasn't ready to discuss his death as a blessing.

The major seemed to feel her shock and turned the subject, blowing his nose on his handkerchief. "Mentioned in dispatches, was Smithers," he said gruffly. "Dashed brave chap. Can't say anything but good of him."

"Perhaps we'd better both make that a rule, Major," said Leonora. "We both care so deeply for Wilhelmina, we might not do justice to the poor man's memory."

"My feelings exactly, ma'am," cried the major.

At this point Esmé came back, of necessity entering through the sitting room, since it boasted the lodgings's only door to the outside. Leonora asked the girl to bring in the claret and remarked, with an apologetic shrug, "I should be glad my chaperon's returned, sir. I'd quite forgotten that we shouldn't have been sitting here alone."

"Nothing in it," said Danforth with a snort. "You're like a sister to me, ma'am." He reddened to the ears.

"We must keep that goal in mind," responded Leonora.

Her knowing look quite finished the major's composure.

CHAPTER FIVE

"WHAT HAVE YOU DONE?" Leonora's tone was sharp.

Wilhelmina bustled and fussed, taking off her bonnet, folding her pelisse, and casting about for her sewing before she sat down opposite Leonora in the parlour window and continued with her story. "I've found a perfectly delightful way to get you into Society, that's all. None of this folderol about waiting for the opening assembly and then having to guard you so that that Forrester person or some other nobody doesn't carry you off to the floor before a worthy suitor has the proper chance. This will make it so much easier for us both. In only a few days you'll be the centre of a charming group of young people."

"How?" Leonora pursued.

"Why, Lady Markham is getting up a scheme of entertainment, and she asked for your help. She must have noticed you particularly, Leonora. It's very flattering to be singled out by Lady Markham. She wouldn't let an unsuitable girl near Lord Stone."

Leonora ignored the reference to Lady Markham's stepson. If Billie had matchmaking ideas about her and that young man, they weren't worth dignifying with her attention. "What do you mean by 'a scheme of entertainment'?"

"Oh . . . nothing to signify. Only think, Leonora. You'll be going in and out of the Markham house every day, and

I shall be, too! I'll go with you as your chaperon. No use to waste entrée to the Markhams' on Esmé."

"Billie, I demand to know what you've got me into," said Leonora. Her eyes flashed.

Her sister quailed before the show of displeasure. "A play," she mumbled.

"A play?" Leonora's voice rose nearly to a shriek. *"A play?"*

"It's simple." Billie's voice rattled on quickly, words tripping over one another as the story spilled out. "Lady Markham is giving private theatricals, for a select audience, and she wishes *you* to be the heroine. Miss Derwent, the girl who was to do it, cried off. Nothing could be more promising, Leonora. You'll be brought to the attention of the members of the ton who have come here for the Season, for Lady Markham knows everyone worth knowing. And your hero will be Lord Stone. What could be more romantic than playing love scenes together? I daresay I'll be making an interesting announcement about you before the play is even ready."

Leonora had dropped her sewing and risen to her feet. She was actually trembling, Billie was amazed to see. "You said I'd act? Upon the stage?"

"It isn't the public stage, my dear. People do it all the time. I remember when I was a child, the vicar's family would put on plays and pantomimes over the Christmas holidays, and you know the dear vicar would never do anything improper. They'd fit up the barn as a playhouse, and it was the greatest amusement. I'm sure you'll love it."

"I won't," said Leonora. "Act the lead in a play, with a pack of strangers? I simply can't. I'll say I'm in mourning for my brother-in-law."

"No! I'm the one who said you could do it, and Edward was my husband. Oh, Leonora. No one here but

Danforth is certain when Edward died. Don't expose me. I know I shouldn't have come out of mourning so soon, but it's been over six months now.'' Billie's large blue eyes filled with tears.

"I'll say I'm ill," was Leonora's next suggestion.

"Lady Markham would never believe it. Leonora, you must do this. Think of me if not yourself. How else am I to get into that household and work my wiles upon Sir Hector?''

"Oh—hire out as a housemaid for all I care. I can't act, Billie." Leonora shuddered at the mere thought.

"You're shy," said Billie. "Well, everyone has stage fright. Once, not long before Badajoz, I had to recite the prologue in a little play one of the officers had written. I was quite good, as it turned out, and when I remember how frightened I was beforehand—''

"No," said Leonora.

The battle of wills continued. Leonora threatened to go home to Papa no matter what the cost to her good name. Billie countered with a threat of tears and followed through. Leonora, not to be moved by dramatics, stalked to her room to pack. Billie followed, crying out about family loyalty and her own pressing desire to marry Sir Hector Markham.

"I'd be established for life, dear. And I could take you to London and present you properly if you're truly not going to consider Lord Stone. Yes, that's much the best thing. I shall marry first and sponsor you in Town. Think of it, Leonora! Almack's, perhaps a court presentation for both of us.''

"Your wits have gone begging, Billie," said Leonora from behind a stack of clean petticoats she was about to throw into an open valise.

"It's such a small thing." Billie was sniffling now. She sat down on Leonora's favourite gown, laid out upon the bed.

Leonora sighed, dropped the petticoats beside Billie, and knelt before her sister. "Dearest, you mustn't dream such very grand dreams. You're bound to be disappointed. How has my taking part in some silly tragedy turned into a court presentation? Sir Hector may not marry you, no matter how much time you spend in his house."

"But I'll have a better chance at him," said Billie. "I'm not so foolish as you think, sister. I've asked questions about Sir Hector, and you may be sure I won't marry him until I'm assured of his income."

"Oh, Billie. Don't you ever think of marrying for love?"

"I did it once, or so I thought, and it didn't serve. I know what I'm about. Please, please say you'll help me." Billie's blue eyes, bright with tears, were quite an affecting sight. "Besides, you're wrong," she added with a timid smile. "This play isn't a tragedy. It's a comedy."

Leonora looked into Billie's face. She wanted nothing less than to help her sister marry Sir Hector Markham. But perhaps ... perhaps Billie would come to her senses if she came to know the gentleman better. Leonora didn't remember much about him. She had met him but once, and a faint memory of an overly familiar manner and bandy legs had stuck in her mind. Surely Major Danforth would look like a prince beside such a man.

"I'm not saying I'll do it, mind you," said Leonora, "but tell me more about this play. Shakespeare?"

"No, it's by an Irish gentleman. A very genteel comedy, I understand, and you are to play a Quakeress. There's nothing unrefined in that, is there?" Billie, her face glowing with happiness, kissed her sister's forehead and ran out into the parlour, in search of the copy of *Wild Oats* she had brought home with her.

"A Quakeress?" Leonora was intrigued in spite of herself. She was soon perusing the hand-copied manuscript with a speculative eye. There were features in the play's favour. As Lady Amaranth, Leonora would indeed be dignified. No flittering about the stage or languishing was called for. No intimacies were written into the stage directions, no kissing or cuddling between her and Lord Stone in the character of Jack Rover.

These factors, together with Billie's eagerness that Leonora take the role and her fear of embarrassment before the ladies of Cheltenham should she not, decided Leonora in favour of trying out the part. She would preserve the option, she told herself, of crying off later as had Miss Derwent before her. A lady might always change her mind.

THE NEXT DAY MISS CLARE was summoned to the Royal Crescent. A curt note from Lady Markham informed the young lady that they must make up for lost time, as her predecessor had been so missish as to cry craven.

Leonora disdained to primp for this outing and looked askance at Billie's extravagant preparations, finally insisting that her sister fill in the low décolletage of her walking dress with a muslin scarf. "You aren't hawking your wares, my dear. Sir Hector already knows you have a nice figure," Leonora said in her most governesslike tone.

"Well, I hate to leave any stone unturned," said Billie, but she agreed tamely enough.

The portals of the Markham house in the Royal Crescent were soon opening to the sisters. The modern houses in the Crescent, a development hard by Billie's own little street near the church, were noted for large, sunny rooms and picturesque bow windows. Lacy iron balconies gave the houses an airy charm.

Leonora had to admit that she was enchanted by the Crescent. Cows were grazing on the grassy enclosure before the curving row of houses on this bright day, and she imagined there must be breathtaking views of the Cotswold Hills from some of the windows of the sparkling dwellings.

Lady Markham's house had a bare elegance which also drew Leonora's favour. Thin and graceful furnishings stood on gleaming parquet floors. Tables and shelves were uncluttered. The only ornaments were some fine pieces of chinoiserie.

"Rather like a tomb, isn't it?" whispered Billie, whose taste was not Leonora's, as the two followed the butler.

He showed them into a roomful of people, none of whom Leonora had met. From Billie's startled look, Leonora inferred that not many of the company were known to her sister, either.

Lady Markham rose from a seat near the unseasonable fire and advanced, the long train of her chintz morning robe dragging behind her. An indoor headdress, consisting of a mob-cap tied under the chin and several feathers, hid most of her grey hair.

Leonora knew when she was in the presence of self-styled royalty. She dropped a small curtsy, no deeper than she would have given any older lady of her own rank, and noticed out of the corner of her eye that Billie was vouchsafing the baronet's widow the full court reverence.

"Miss Clare. And Mrs.—er—Smithers. Delightful. You've brought the manuscript, I see, young lady. We are all waiting for you."

Leonora peeked at the small watch pinned to the bosom of her gown. They were exactly on time. "My lady, we must have mistaken the hour," she said sweetly.

The steely eyes of Lady Markham met Leonora's for an instant. A silent "touché" passed between them.

"Humph," was all Lady Markham said. "Well, now you *are* here, there's plenty of work to do. I assume you know everyone?"

"No, ma'am, I'm newly arrived in Cheltenham and haven't made much acquaintance," was Leonora's demure reply. She would evidently have to do all the talking for herself and her sister. How distressing, she thought, that the mere sight of a lady who was of no higher rank than their late mother should turn Billie into a mute!

The necessity of introductions seemed to annoy Lady Markham, but there was no help for it. She could scarcely ask Miss Clare to sit down and read with strangers. She had already decided that she approved of the girl, though Miss Clare's true colours remained to be shown. Acting would bring out her mettle, if mettle she had. Quite evident already was the fact that Leonora Clare was nothing like her sister. That, thought Lady Markham with a sniff in the direction of the vulgar Widow Smithers, was an advantage.

The company stood up or nodded, according to their sex. Lady Markham made the introductions short and sweet. "Lady Cecilia Crawe, Mr. Hampton, Ensign Derwent—whose sister could not perform in your role; Miss Pickering—" The names passed by Leonora and were forgotten as quickly. She would ask Billie about her fellow actors later. "You have met my stepson, I believe? Lord Stone," finished Lady Markham as a young man rushed into the room and came to an abrupt stop in front of the ladies.

So, Leonora thought, the company had not been waiting only for her. She made her curtsy to a thin young man with a shock of brown hair, large watery eyes, no chin to speak of, and a foppish suit of clothes. Did Billie think any woman of sense would marry this specimen? Hiding a smile, Leonora acknowledged their one brief meeting at church the other day.

"Ah! And here comes Brother Hector. He's to do Farmer Gammon."

Leonora turned towards the door and the other latecomer, eager to behold again the man her sister had designed for her future brother-in-law. Sir Hector strode in. "Well, well, dear Mrs. Smithers, brought your little sister, I hear." The baronet bowed over Billie's hand. Leonora thought he leered. Then he turned to her.

"Miss Clare. Enchanted to see you again. Overwhelmed." Sir Hector's thin lips curved in a wolfish smile. He was, as Leonora had remembered, a man chiefly remarkable for his thin and inelegant legs, which he chose to encase in skin-tight pantaloons. His narrow face was attractive enough, widened by a judicious crop of sidewhiskers. He was dressed in the same extravagant style as his nephew by marriage: coat with obviously padded shoulders and nipped-in waist, waistcoat of startling hue, and tassled Hessians so highly polished that Leonora, if she had cared to, might have seen her face in them. She wondered if Sir Hector ever gazed at his own visage in the mirrors of his boots. He struck her as the sort of fribble who might take pleasure in such an affectation.

She murmured her greetings, wondering how she would ever be able to keep a straight face in this company. Luckily the play was to be a comedy! And aside from Sir Hector and Lord Stone, the cast looked to be composed of harmless people.

"How droll you are, brother," said Lady Markham, which put a period to Sir Hector's gallantry. "Shall we all take our seats and begin? Oh. Mrs. Smithers. You may sit in that corner with Miss Pickering's chaperon."

Leonora glanced at the window seat her ladyship had indicated. A quietly dressed woman with a bored expression, a governess or a maid, was waiting. Leonora felt she could not allow Billie to be shoved aside in such a way. "I particularly need my sister to prompt me," she said, grasping Billie's hand and making for a vacant sofa.

Lady Markham looked down her aristocratic nose, but there was little she could say in retort without appearing as rude as she had no doubt intended to be. Clearing her throat, the lady made her way to her thronelike chair and rattled her manuscript.

There was no preliminary summary of the plot. Leonora was much aware of having come in on the middle of the project. A cursory read-through had helped her outline the basic story: a young man had run away from home to join a troupe of strolling players. Among them was his friend, the consummate actor Jack Rover, a man who found his words in the words of others: his every line was a quotation from another play. The leading role of Rover ought to be played by someone with flair, certainly someone other than that prosaic mumbler, Lord Stone, thought Leonora, seeing what hash the young baron made of a mere reading of his lines.

The action was quick and complex. In the end Jack Rover, revealed as the elder brother of the young runaway and thus the heir to an estate, won the hand of Quakerish Lady Amaranth. On the way a false marriage was proved genuine, a mother met her son, and Jack Rover, whimsical though he sometimes was, stood revealed as an honest and unselfish man.

"Louder, Poynton," said Lady Markham at one point, when her son had muttered one line too many into the paper in front of him. "Take your cue from Miss Clare. You have a nice voice, gel. Carrying."

Billie squeezed her sister's hand at this sign of Lady Markham's approval. Leonora knew that Billie must be mentally designing wedding clothes by this time.

When the reading was over Lady Markham herded the group into the morning room to partake of a cold collation. The airy parlour, with its high windows looking out to the hills, was a most pleasant place. Fruit and meat were set out on a table in the centre of the room, and the players were urged to help themselves and find seats.

Leonora picked up a roll of bread and a peach, placed them on a plate, and contemplated her next move. She was astonished to find Lord Stone at her side.

"Mama says I'm to learn from you," the young man said brightly.

His shy smile would have softened Leonora's heart in other circumstances, but as it was, she didn't care in the least to be kind to him and raise her sister's hopes.

"I have no experience, and I can't imagine what I could teach you," she responded.

"How to make my voice carry," explained Lord Stone.

His voice would likely carry far if she were to step on his foot with all her strength, Leonora thought in a moment of humour. But she would save that manoeuvre for more desperate circumstances.

Seeing Miss Pickering alone in a corner, she excused herself to Lord Stone and approached the girl. Billie was busy talking with Sir Hector, and to Leonora none of the other strangers in the room looked half so likely to need her help as this young creature. Lady Markham had made the girl cry when she'd lost her place in the reading. Miss

Pickering, a pretty child with soft brown curls and china-blue eyes, was wiping her nose and looking quite forlorn.

"Oh, how do you do, Miss Clare?" she said, glancing up timidly. "Oh!" More tears welled up. "I've made such a muddle of things."

Leonora sat down by the other girl and began to repair Lady Markham's damage. "If you mean losing your place that one time, don't give it another thought. Why, Lady Markham has scolded everyone in this room at least once."

"Except you," murmured the girl, looking up at Leonora with a worshipful expression.

"She simply didn't find the time," said Leonora. She wished Lady Markham *had* criticized her, for it would be uncomfortable to be seen as her ladyship's pet. "I was going to suggest, Miss Pickering, that we might meet to rehearse together if you feel the need."

"Oh, that would be famous, ma'am," said the girl at once. "And please do call me Portia."

"And you must call me Leonora."

"I was thinking of crying off," Portia confided, with a shy glance at the daunting figure of Lady Markham across the room. "But Mama would never allow it. She thinks I must make the most of this chance to snag Lord Stone."

"Heavens, is everyone in Cheltenham thinking the same thing? My sister wishes *me* to catch him."

Once such a bond was established, the young ladies were assured of forming a friendship. They decided to walk home together.

Billie's sharp eyes, busy though they had been shooting sly darts at Sir Hector during the meal, had missed nothing. She was not best pleased that Leonora had left the side of an obviously besotted Lord Stone in order to talk to a female, but quick was the consolation that Portia was the daughter of a very respectable family.

Mrs. Smithers was cheerful enough as she walked between the two young ladies down the Crescent, Portia's mama's maid trailing behind them. Leonora and her sister soon learned that Portia was only seventeen and hadn't yet had a Season. The production of *Wild Oats* was her first foray into adult Society.

"Mama is quite frugal," she admitted with a shrug. "I suppose she thinks that if I marry Lord Stone, she won't have the expense of a come-out."

Billie's eyes narrowed upon hearing the chit was on the catch for Stone, but a moment's reflection brought her back to good humour. How could this insignificant little thing compare with Leonora?

"My goodness," whispered Portia suddenly, "what a very handsome man!"

Leonora looked up. Mr. Richard Forrester was approaching them along the pavement. He was smiling.

She smiled back, sensing, though she did not look, that Billie's expression was not half so welcoming.

Luckily, Forrester wasn't put off by Mrs. Smithers's version of the cut direct. He walked up to the trio, doffing a high-crowned beaver which was somewhat the worse for wear.

Billie had put on an awful frown, and she wasn't holding out her hand. Leonora defiantly gave Forrester her own.

"Miss Clare! I've been wondering how I could manage to see you again. Stalking the country lanes hasn't helped."

Leonora dimpled with pleasure at the compliment. "I notice, sir, that your ankle seems to be cured."

Forrester didn't miss a beat. "Ah, yes. Soaked it in the waters. Good as new."

Leonora looked at him archly but said nothing more on that dangerous subject.

"We must be going, Mr. Forrester," Billie said. "If you will excuse us?"

"Mrs. Smithers! At last you address me. How promising." Forrester's eyes held a teasing glint as he bowed to the widow.

Billie made an incoherent sound of fury.

Miss Pickering's face drooped. She must have realized that she was not to be presented to this charming man. With large and wistful eyes, she watched him walk away.

"Billie!" said Leonora as soon as he was a safe distance down the pavement. "Must you be so rude?"

"Yes. It's the only thing which will counteract your shameless encouragement of that man."

Miss Pickering asked, "Is he not well-born, ma'am. Or is he poor?"

The innocent question nearly made Leonora laugh. Her new friend Portia, young though she was, had a grip on what Society thought important. One did not need a come-out, then, to learn the ways of the world.

Billie smiled wisely on the young girl. "We don't know what he is, dear. That's the trouble. And what could be more dangerous than a handsome man one knows nothing about? I can see your mother has taught you to be cautious. Perhaps you can help Leonora learn from your example."

"From *my* example?" gasped the ingénue.

"To be sure, my dear. If that man should get into the assembly, for instance, I'm sure *you* wouldn't dance with him."

Leonora glared at her sister, and she resolved on the spot to dance with Mr. Forrester at the assembly if she had the good fortune to be asked.

"I'm certain he wouldn't ask me," Portia said with a sigh.

"Hmm." Billie considered this carefully. The matronly pose she had adopted required some sensible answer. "And no more *should* he ask you," she pronounced. "You haven't been introduced." In her tone was the suggestion that she had not performed that introduction solely out of regard for the young lady's safety.

"Leonora?" Portia turned an eager look on her new friend.

Leonora gave a noncommittal shrug. She wouldn't tease Billie by promising to present the unsuitable Forrester to Miss Pickering.

Besides, she was more than half inclined to keep the man to herself.

CHAPTER SIX

"No, Lord Eldon," said Leonora in a raised voice, respectful of his lordship's difficult hearing, "I will not sit upon your knee. May I serve you coffee or tea?"

"Another cup o' this punch is more like, m'dear. Don't get up. I'll fetch it m'self."

The elderly peer rose from his place beside Leonora and toddled across the sitting-room to the corner where punch and glasses were laid out on a table as rickety as he.

Leonora, presiding over the tea-tray at her sister's soirée, surveyed the room. She was beginning to think it would serve Billie well if one of these old hobgoblins did marry her. In an excess of discomfort, Leonora promised herself she would keep to her room at Billie's next party.

She knew in her heart, though, even as she made that vow, that she would do the same thing she was doing at this very moment: appear, so that she might lend some small countenance to her sister's otherwise all-masculine gathering.

Billie was standing at the centre of a group of three men: two "old titles," as Leonora privately called Billie's suitors, and Major Danforth. The dashing Mrs. Smithers had on the one mourning gown she liked: an extremely low-cut black gauze, trimmed in jet beads, which a colonel's lady in Spain had given her. Leonora knew her sister wore the dress not out of respect for her dead husband, but because it was so particularly becoming.

Billie was standing because so many of her admirers required chairs if they were to bear late hours. It was eight o'clock. The plush sofa, the brocade armchair, and the balding velvet long chair were dotted with gentlemen, middle-aged and old. Each had given Leonora a trial, addressing suggestive remarks to her in the style they used to her sister. Her cold and disapproving manner had repelled each would-be dallier in turn, but once in a while someone would try again, as Lord Eldon just had.

Then there was the youngest, and, in Leonora's opinion, the only dangerous gentleman of the group. She found herself confronted now by Sir Hector Markham.

"Dearest Miss Clare, if you could give me tea?" The suave voice was too near her ear. "May I say how lovely you are looking tonight?"

"Thank you," said Leonora in an ironic tone. She did not look in the least lovely. She had chosen an unseasonably warm dark brown merino gown precisely because it made her look a quiz and was not proper evening dress, in order to emphasize her self-appointed role of chaperon at these parties.

"How delightful it will be to be more in your company since you have consented to act in my sister-in-law's play, fair lady," continued Sir Hector. His eyebrows wiggled about alarmingly.

"Quite," said Leonora. "Your tea, sir." She moved to hand over a Staffordshire cup which was only a little chipped. Her hand shook. "Oh!" she cried in genuine dismay. She might dislike the man, but she had no wish to anger him. "I do beg your pardon. Your lovely breeches."

Sir Hector surveyed the brown splash of tea Leonora had spilled near the knee of his sparkling white satin smallclothes. "It's no matter, my dear," he said with determined chivalry, dabbing at the spot with a handkerchief.

Leonora let fall several more remarks expressive of her great contrition.

"I assure you, dear lady, these breeches are nothing— less than nothing," Sir Hector proclaimed. He gave her a significant look. "And it's surely quite improper for us to be discussing my, er, garments."

"You are correct, sir," Leonora said with modestly downcast eyes. She wondered if he could be playing the proper and upright gentleman in order to slip past her defences. He would catch cold at that game.

Sir Hector seemed about to say something else when a commotion at the door distracted him. A flurry of high-pitched Spanish filled the room as Esmé struggled to hold the front door closed. A booted foot stayed her progress.

"Heavens!" Billie hurried to the door. "Whomever are you keeping out, Esmé?"

Major Danforth, straightening his shoulders, followed Mrs. Smithers in the spirit of chivalrous support.

"Mrs. Smithers!" called a deep voice.

Leonora felt her heartbeat quicken. She would know that voice anywhere. Forrester!

Billie had also recognized the resonant tones. "Go away, you dreadful man," she cried through the door.

"I know the *señora* not like this one," Esmé proclaimed, turning from the scene. She gathered a tray of empty glasses and disappeared into the pantry, casting one last stormy glance in the direction of the door.

"Mrs. Smithers, please. I lay no claim on your hospitality, but I bring you a guest: Lord Carlisle."

"Oh!" Billie exchanged a look with Major Danforth.

Lord Carlisle happened to be Billie's favourite candidate for marriage, after Sir Hector.

Billie and Major Danforth released pressure on the door.

Forrester nearly fell into the room. In his strong arms he bore Lord Carlisle, a frail, bewigged man of about eighty summers. A footman, wheeling his lordship's Bath chair, followed in his wake.

"Devil of a time getting that thing up the stairs," said Forrester cheerfully. "There you go, m'lord."

"Much obliged, young man," said Carlisle in a creaking voice. "Manners of the old school. Better than some of these modern lads." He cast a baleful eye round the room, causing several fifty-year-old guests to squirm like guilty schoolboys.

"My lord," spoke up Sir Hector Markham, "naturally we assumed that your servants would be bringing you."

"Assumed!" fumed the old man. "Didn't ask, though, did ye, if I'd care to go about with someone besides m'footmen?"

Sir Hector had no answer to make, so he bowed.

Billie greeted Lord Carlisle in her most effusive manner. She glanced at Forrester, and Leonora could almost hear her sister thinking. How could she eject from her lodgings the companion of her prey, Lord Carlisle?

Forrester, grinning, forced the issue. "Now that I've performed my commission, Mrs. Smithers, I take my leave." He made a charming bow and even dared a wistful look about at the scene of merriment.

"What? What?" cried Carlisle. "You'll stay, young man. Any friend of mine's a friend of Mrs. Smithers, ain't that so, m'dear?" The last words were spoken with a leer at Billie.

Billie seemed to wilt as she said, in a resigned voice, "Certainly, my lord. Mr. Forrester, you are welcome, if a quiet sort of entertainment such as this—"

"It's a perfect entertainment, as any occasion must be which includes yourself and your sister," said Forrester, sweeping another bow. "Now I leave his lordship in your capable hands, madam. Perhaps Miss Clare would give me tea."

Billie turned her back on Forrester, ostensibly to devote herself to Lord Carlisle. But before she did, she gave Leonora her severest warning stare.

Leonora paid no attention. She was all admiration that Forrester had managed to worm his way into her sister's home.

"Well met, Miss Clare." He approached with an intimate smile. "You might as well pour me some tea, but I'll confess that my purpose in coming here was simply to be by your side."

Unfortunately, that side was still tenanted by Sir Hector Markham. Drawing out a quizzing glass, this gentleman gave Forrester a thorough inspection, letting his gaze linger on the frayed cuffs of the younger man's blue coat and the telling limpness of his linen. "Have we met, sir?"

Forrester shrugged. "I meet so many people. It's quite possible. White's, perhaps? The name is Forrester."

Sir Hector murmured, "Forrester? Can't say I recall. So you are a member of White's, sir?" Again he gave Forrester a measuring look, as though gauging his honesty as well as the shabbiness of his attire. "Most unusual. You seem on friendly terms indeed with this young lady, Forrester, and without her sister's wholehearted approval, if I may be so bold."

Forrester winked. "I had to storm the castle, in fact. I don't believe I caught your name?"

Leonora conducted the formal introduction, wishing she dared to spill a whole pot of tea on Sir Hector in order to rid herself of him.

Luckily he was hailed by another gentleman, and Forrester and Leonora were left comparatively alone.

"What do you think of my ingenuity, ma'am?" he asked.

"My sister must certainly revise her opinion of Lord Carlisle's intimate friend," said Leonora demurely.

"Oh, as to that: we met at the Pump Room the other day and struck up an acquaintance. Comparing ailments, don't you know."

Leonora smiled. "Somehow I doubt you have a great deal in common—physically—with Lord Carlisle."

"Ah, ma'am, let's not mire ourselves in the subject of illness on this festive occasion," Forrester said with a sigh. "Tell me about some of the guests, if you would. I'm a stranger hereabouts, as you know, and I ought to make the most of this opportunity to attend an evening party."

Leonora did not hesitate. "It ought to be obvious even to a fool, which you are not, that my sister is trying to hook one of these old reprobates." She spoke in a lowered voice and leaned towards Forrester. "While you will meet nothing but titles here, you are doing your own consequence no good by being seen at Mrs. Smithers's."

Forrester gave a delighted grin as he accepted a cup of tea from Leonora's hand. "How honest you are, ma'am. A refreshing change. Is Sir Hector Markham in your sister's court or yours?"

"I don't know the gentleman well, but I suspect he plays the gallant to many women," said Leonora, thinking of his leading comments about the discussion of breeches. Sir Hector would definitely bear watching. She was in no danger, but Billie might find herself in the briars if the baronet decided to add her seduction to his social calendar. "Perhaps it's merely old-fashioned courtliness?"

"The manoeuvrings of a desperate rake, more like. I see he's hovering about your sister now."

Leonora preferred not to dwell on the fact that Sir Hector was indeed draped across the back of Billie's chair, which that lady had positioned near Lord Carlisle. "That situation does worry me, sir, but I see no way to check it. Shall we talk of something else?"

"Let us talk of your beauty and charm, my dear young lady," was Forrester's instant response. "After all, these qualities of yours were my motivation for this evening's manoeuvrings."

Leonora's hand shook, and her cup clinked revealingly in its saucer. She returned in desperation to a safer, though less flattering, subject. "Sir Hector and his family seem to be the ruling force hereabouts."

"I've heard of them, now you mention it. Hasn't he a sister-in-law who takes the local social life by the throat and shakes it?"

Leonora giggled. "Lady Markham is rather forceful."

"She has a son, I believe?" Forrester's tone was casual, and he stifled a yawn.

"A stepson. Lord Stone. A-an interesting young man."

"Indeed?" Forrester gave Leonora a piercing look. "Do you know anything more about the family? The stepson—Lord Stone—seems to be but very recently come into his title. And nobody that I can find ever saw or heard of him before he inherited from his unfortunate military brother."

"My sister and I are strangers here; we know nothing about the local families," Leonora said. "Do you have a special interest in these people?" Here, perhaps, was the clue to Forrester's own mysterious lack of a past. Major Danforth knew him, yes; but not another soul in Cheltenham seemed to have heard of him.

Forrester shrugged, dashing Leonora's hopes of a revealing disclosure. "I wouldn't say so. I am a student of human nature, ma'am, and I find it interesting in all its particulars. A mysterious baron is bound to fascinate me. There are so few real mysteries in life.''

''I simply cannot think of Lord Stone as mysterious,'' Leonora said with a laugh. ''I would guess that his retiring nature kept him living a quiet life until his stepmother insisted he bestir himself. The young man has become a matrimonial prize of sorts, you see, since he inherited his title, and her ladyship doubtless wishes to display him.''

Forrester nodded seriously in response to this. ''Logical. Flawlessly logical,'' he said. ''I do see what you mean by Lady Markham's desire to put her son—her stepson— on display. He is your fellow player, I think?''

''You've heard about the theatricals.'' Leonora shrugged. ''I was pressed into service, but I will admit the project has introduced me to many people. Lady Markham's cast seems to include most of the population of Cheltenham. I don't know whom she'll invite to make up the audience.''

Forrester laughed. ''Me, I hope. I'll have to get into the lady's good graces.''

''I wish you luck there, sir,'' replied Leonora. She was interrupted then, by another gentleman wishing tea, and Forrester wandered off. Leonora looked after him, wondering if he had elbowed his way into Billie's party purely as a lark—for he seemed a most whimsical man—or whether he wished to be with Leonora as much as he said.

THE NEXT EVENING WAS THE Season's first assembly ball. The sisters spent most of the afternoon in preparation.

Billie was more relieved than she let Leonora know, for she had the great Mr. King's assurance that she and her sister would be welcome in the rooms that evening. She had been worried that rumours of her former raffishness

might exclude them both. Luckily, the Master of Ceremonies had heard that Leonora was intimate with Lady
Markham and had assured Mrs. Smithers that he would
delight in seeing her, and Miss Clare, in his preserve of
elegance.

Leonora, who hadn't an idea that they might have been
refused admittance, tried in vain to dissuade Billie from
wearing the striking black evening gown. "Since you
haven't been appearing in mourning regularly, it might
look odd," she ventured. Her sister would stand out in the
crowd for a certainty in that diaphanous, sparkling crea-
tion, and Leonora intended to prevent it if she could.

"Everyone will understand that I only recently came out
of mourning. My dear, I don't own anything else half so
becoming. I bought my last ball gown in the year eight,"
said Billie, rummaging in a bandbox full of fripperies.
"Now where did I put that paste clip? Ah!" She drew forth
a large, false diamond brooch which she proceeded to attach to the black satin bandeau ornamenting her hair. A
couple of lavender feathers completed the headdress.

"Well, you must promise me you won't dance if you insist on going about in your blacks," Leonora said. Even as
she kept the conversation on the question of propriety, as
the best means of bringing Billie round, she worried that
the black gown spoke more of dalliance than of mourning.

Billie only laughed. "Hadn't you better dress, sister?"

"I might as well not bother. No one will see me next to
you," grumbled Leonora.

Billie, assuming this was a sisterly show of jealousy, was
even more satisfied with her appearance.

Leonora had brought one ball gown with her, a pale
green figured silk with an overlay of white tissue. The last
and only time she had worn it, one gentleman had likened

her to a mermaid. She noticed, as she surveyed her reflection in her small bedroom glass, that her gown was nearly as low-necked as Billie's. Ought she to feel guilty for having chided her sister? Leonora emerged into the sitting-room eventually, ready down to the simple white fan dangling from her wrist, and still unsettled on this point. She decided not to bring up the subject.

Major Danforth, resplendent in full military regalia, arrived to escort them. At precisely the proper hour they walked into the Assembly Rooms in the High Street, there to be greeted by Mr. King and taken to sign the book.

"And now," said that courtly gentleman, "there is someone who has been waiting to meet you ladies. Someone whom I'm sure you'll delight in finding here. Ah! Here he is."

Leonora turned eagerly, expecting Forrester. Instead she found herself looking into a pair of red-latticed pale blue eyes set in a countenance she knew only too well.

"Papa!" she gasped.

CHAPTER SEVEN

LEONORA STOOD GAPING at her father. A palpable tension emanated from Billie. What would happen now? Would Billie shriek, faint, or otherwise disgrace them all?

But Billie proved that she had indeed learned courage in her years with the army. "How do you do, Father?" she said with a brief nod. Then she turned on her heel and walked away on the arm of Major Danforth, the latter looking over his shoulder in awful fascination.

Leonora, much as she deplored Billie's desertion, knew it was for the best. She found her tongue.

"I'm surprised to see you, Papa."

"You're comin' home with me, young woman. Was that Billie? Plump as a partridge; older, too. I can't have you mixing with the ragtag and bobtail she's picked up. I've heard stories, Leonora. Been here only since the afternoon, but I know a thing or two."

The father and daughter were standing in the entrance portico, an island in a sea of elegant ladies and gentlemen who must pass by them en route to the main hall. Mr. King, after bringing the family together, had wandered off about his duties. Leonora thanked the stars that the powerful master of ceremonies was not by to observe her father very near to shouting at her.

"Please moderate your voice, Papa," she said. Sir John's eyes were bulging, and one could easily fancy steam issuing from his ears. "We wouldn't wish to cause talk."

Sir John grabbed his daughter's elbow. "You'll come with me. A stop by that trollop's den to pick up your clothes, then off we go to Wiltshire. I've a postchaise waiting."

Leonora fought down a sensation of panic. She might assert that she was her own mistress, but until recently she had obeyed her father as a matter of course. She was a dutiful daughter, and he had never tested that duty to the limits before. But now, she reminded herself, he had.

"I'm glad to hear you've got rid of the new cook, Papa," she said with a smile. "I know you wouldn't expect me to come home if you hadn't done so. My good name would never survive living in the same house with such a woman."

"What? Give Rosie the sack? My habits have nothing to do with you, girl, and you shan't meddle in my affairs. The devil! Lettin' my own daughter dictate to me. Not likely," said Sir John. He had softened his voice somewhat, but the note of rage was still clear in it.

Leonora sighed, averting her eyes from her father's angry face. "Sir, I've come to the assembly with my sister, and I propose to attend it. And you can't order me about. I have my income from Aunt Felicity. I can go where I will."

Sir John raged, still blessedly in an undertone, "Obey me or lose your dowry! Felicity's mite won't buy you a husband of any Quality." He tightened his hold on his daughter's arm.

Leonora froze. Was brute force to carry the day? She cared less than nothing for her dowry, but could she cause a scene by saying so? She stood in confusion, for she had to admit that, whatever his vagaries, she still loved her father. A complete breach was imminent, she sensed, and she would regret that mightily.

Someone stopped in their path, and a hearty voice said, in cheerful tones, "You must be the famous Sir John Clare. Didn't you have a horse run at Epsom last year? I'm pleased to make your acquaintance." A large, gloved hand landed on Sir John's burly shoulder, and Leonora looked up, relieved, into the face of Richard Forrester.

Forrester had never looked better. Though his evening coat was worn and his pumps, upon close inspection, somewhat down at heel, his auburn hair shone bright in the candlelight, and he gazed on Leonora with a tender expression which might have embarrassed her under other circumstances. Now she was only grateful to him for seeing the situation at a glance—for saving her.

Sir John had to stop and acknowledge the stranger, and he released his hold on his daughter's arm. She stepped a safe distance away.

"Richard Forrester, sir. At your service," said the younger man with a bow. "May I have this dance? With your daughter, I mean to say. And allow me to congratulate you, sir, on the beauty of your two daughters. Take after their mother, do they?"

Leonora eagerly stepped to Forrester's side and accepted his arm. Her eyes glinted in mischief as she saw how her father was gaping at this outrageous young man. She made a motion of her head to Forrester, and he took her cue and hurried her off into the ballroom.

"Here's room for us," he said into her ear, steering her to a line of dancers. Both sighed in relief.

Leonora took a moment to cast her eyes about. This was her first Cheltenham assembly, and she might as well try to enjoy it. She was with Forrester, just as she had hoped she would be, and that must outweigh, for the moment, the fact that Sir John had come to Cheltenham. The ballroom was pleasant, if a little cramped for the number of dancers. Crystal chandeliers and a musicians' gallery ornamented the large chamber, and the main doorway was decorated with pilasters in the Greek style.

The company gave Leonora the same impression she had had at church the other day: much of fashion, of sophistication, was represented in this room. It seemed odd that Cheltenham, stuck in an inconvenient corner of the kingdom, far from London, should be the goal of all these people.

She tried to set her mind on enjoying the moment. For the first time in her life she was at a public assembly in a popular spa town, mixing with the élite of the fashionable world. She must not think of what her father might have planned for her when the set was over.

"What, thoughtful? Can it be you're not pleased to see your rather choleric-looking parent?" asked Forrester, smiling down at her. Rather than getting into line, in formation for the dance, he was keeping close by her side.

"Papa has come to take me home to Wiltshire," said Leonora with a sigh. "And since I won't go, he'll be in a rage. I do wish..." She hesitated. "This will sound quite odd, but I wish he would stay in Cheltenham. He might become reconciled to my sister—and she to him."

"Perhaps we can persuade him to stay on to taste the delights of Cheltenham in the Season. He looks as though he could use the waters. Good for spleen, aren't they? Look over there, Miss Clare. He seems to have met some acquaintance."

Leonora did look. Sir John had entered the ballroom, and now he stood deep in conversation with several gentlemen of about his own age. She had forgotten that her papa, with his many visits to London and the racing centres, would no doubt meet people he knew in a place which attracted so many tonnish visitors. She glanced at Forrester. "Don't they have races here in Cheltenham?"

"Capital idea. Certain to attract your sire. Yes, we'll think of something to keep him here. So he doesn't get on with your sister?"

"He cast her off when she married, and he's angry with me for visiting her," said Leonora in such a low tone that no one but Forrester heard her. That was all they had time to say before the music struck up and they were called to their duties as dancers.

When they met during one of the figures, Forrester gave Leonora a wink and said, "Sir John has gone to the cardroom with some cronies. I shouldn't be surprised if he were secure for the whole evening. Is he a card-playing man?"

"Papa?" Leonora stared, wondering how any soul could doubt such an obvious truth, then remembered that Forrester had only just met her parent. "He ought to be happy if only there are some flats among the party. Papa loves a good win."

Forrester nodded sagely as they were obliged again to separate.

On the next turn, Forrester had taken his mind from his partner's father and was back in his usual gallant form. "I quite forgot to mention it in all the excitement, Miss Clare, but you are lovelier than ever tonight. That gown turns your eyes to green."

"Thank you," said Leonora. She also had put her father from her mind, but another matter was troubling her, so much so that she quite failed to take full pleasure in the compliment. Suddenly she felt compelled to share her troubles. She had remarked early on in their acquaintance her odd tendency to confess all to this gentleman, and strange was the knowledge that she didn't mind it at all. "Mr. Forrester, I hate to turn the subject when it's flattering to me, but I am in need of your advice. You know that I'm promised to perform in Lady Markham's play?''

"Lady Amaranth, the virtuous Quakeress," said Forrester with a smile.

Leonora wondered anew at the sources of information open to him. "My difficulty is that the very thought of acting fills me with horror," she stated.

"But you seemed so composed at the first reading."

Leonora's eyes widened. "You weren't there, sir."

"Others were, and they admired your aplomb."

"My composure isn't at issue. I simply don't wish to act." Leonora gave Forrester a look of appeal, quite as if he were the one she would have to convince of that fact.

"There is a simple solution to your problem, ma'am. Tell Lady Markham."

Forrester's cheery words were the last before he was again carried away by the demands of the dance.

Leonora shook her head at such simple logic. It was quite evident that, whatever else Forrester might have found out about Cheltenham Society and Leonora's own business, he hadn't met Lady Markham.

She could glimpse the lady, seated on the sidelines. Wearing an odd, antique-looking gown of stiff brocade and an astonishing headdress of amethysts and flowers stuck into a turban as if at random, Lady Markham was fixing the dancers with a gimlet eye. On closer inspection, Leonora decided Lady Markham was concentrating that disapproving glare on her stepson, Lord Stone, who was fumbling his way through the steps in the company of a white-gowned chit. Or was it Sir Hector who had the lady's malignant attention? He was dancing quite nearby, with—

"Oh, dear," said Leonora under her breath. Billie had taken the floor with Sir Hector Markham. The baronet was at this moment leering at Billie's too-scanty bodice.

"Something amiss, Miss Clare?" It was Forrester again. Hadn't he left her elbow but two seconds before? Leonora chided herself for dreaming through the dance.

"My sister is dancing, and she's dressed in mourning," she said.

"No one but the highest sticklers would blame her," said Forrester. "And I saw her partner—Sir Hector, isn't it?—talking to Mr. King. Must have got permission."

"Is there anything you don't see?" Leonora asked.

"Your heart, Miss Clare. Your heart," was the suave reply, as the music took him away again.

Once the lilting strains of the country dance were over, Forrester gave Leonora his arm and escorted her about the room. "I don't know where to take you," he said. "Not to your father; and your sister is surrounded by a lot of old parties who wouldn't amuse you. How about this Lady Markham? Wouldn't she like to take her leading actress in charge? And you might take the opportunity to tell her you don't wish to be in her play."

Leonora shuddered. "No. Please, sir..." But it was too late. Forrester was already propelling Leonora in her ladyship's direction.

"Miss Clare," said Lady Markham. She peered at the young lady's escort. "Kind of you to come and speak to me. Who are you, young man? Look familiar. Where is my glass?" She began to excavate her reticule as she continued to fix Forrester with a curious stare. "I'm a bit short-sighted," Lady Markham went on. Her hand came out of her bag empty. "Drat! I don't have it. Your name sir?"

"Forrester, an' it please your ladyship," said that gentleman, executing his deepest bow.

"Humph," said Lady Markham. "A very pretty fellow, ain't you? I can't think where I've seen you, Forrester, but it will come to me."

"I hope it does, my lady," responded Forrester. "I sincerely hope it does."

Leonora smiled to herself, wondering if Forrester bore some slight resemblance to another gentleman of the lady's acquaintance. Could two such specimens as Forrester possibly exist in England?

She started from her musings when she realized that both Lady Markham and Forrester were looking at her expectantly.

"Well, girl?" Lady Markham asked sharply. "This lad claims you've something to tell me."

"About the play," prompted Forrester with a wink.

Leonora looked at him in dismay. She couldn't possibly... Glancing at Lady Markham's stern visage, Leonora knew that she would perform in a hundred plays before she found the courage to tell this lady that she did not desire a role in *Wild Oats*.

"I wanted to thank you, my lady, for thinking of me," said Leonora, with modestly downcast eyes. When she raised them, it was to regard Forrester with a private look of vexation.

"Humph. You're a lucky find, as it turns out, miss. A clear voice. A rare talent among the mumblers I'm stuck with. That Miss Pickering, for instance! The ninny can't even keep her place on the page. Had to tell her to write a *Q* next to her lines. And how am I to teach her a country accent if I can't hear her in the first place?"

"Miss Pickering and I have engaged to practise together," said Leonora, hiding the indignation she felt at poor little Portia being discussed in such terms.

"Ah! Good for you. And let me tell you this—"

Whatever communication Lady Markham might have made was never revealed, for at that moment a beefy hand was clamped down on Leonora's shoulder and a harsh voice uttered, "So you danced once; now it's time to be gone. Chaise is waiting."

"Papa!" Leonora proved by her smile of pleasure that she did own some thespian talents. She had forgotten about her surly parent. A glance at Forrester told her that she had an ally.

"Come along." Sir John glared from under beetling brows.

Leonora had an inspiration. "Lady Markham, may I present my father, Sir John Clare. Papa, do tell her ladyship about your plan to take me back to Wiltshire tonight. I'm certain it will amuse her." She paused, enjoying Lady Markham's air of grim displeasure as well as Papa's ill-concealed rage. "Now if all of you will excuse me, I must withdraw to repair a flounce."

She turned her back and walked sedately away, willing Papa not to follow her. He didn't, and Leonora knew why.

Lady Markham's commanding voice was very clear. "Sir, you're mighty high-handed if you think..."

Leonora giggled as she continued her retreat and Lady Markham's voice grew fainter, but no less determined.

"Miss Clare, a splendid manoeuvre," said Forrester.

"Thank you," she said modestly, not surprised to find him walking beside her.

"Now." He held out his hand. "Will you give me a second dance? It might be well to get to the other side of the room before those two discover that your dress doesn't have any flounces."

Leonora allowed herself to be persuaded. This assembly might yet hold pleasures!

CHAPTER EIGHT

WHEN LEONORA AWOKE the morning after the assembly, vague feelings of imminent disaster were intermingled in her mind with the more pleasant image of Richard Forrester. Odd, she thought through a fog, that Forrester should conjure up any but delightful feelings. He had been so gallant last evening, so perfectly charming....

Then she remembered. Swinging her legs over the side of the bed, she pushed the heavy waves of her hair off her forehead. "Papa is here. What can I do?"

It would take next to no time for Papa to be shown the way to Billie's. Noticing how brightly the sun shone in at her little window, and how high above the horizon, Leonora wondered why Sir John hadn't stormed in already.

Heavens, could she have slept through a family brawl? Throwing a light shawl about the shoulders of her cambric nightdress, she hurried to the sitting room, fully expecting some scene of carnage. Instead there was only Billie, looking very sleepy under a lace nightcap. The widow was half-enveloped in a Chinese dressing-gown of scarlet silk, a robe which had evidently belonged to a man—her husband, it was to be hoped.

Billie looked up. "Oh, there you are. Esmé will be bringing breakfast soon. How delightfully rested you look, my dear."

Leonora sat. "Billie, you were magnificent last night when you met Papa. Like a queen."

"If you want the truth, love, I've been considering for years what I'd say if I saw Papa again," said Billie in an airy tone.

"It was perfect. Aren't you worried that he will come here?"

"Not for the moment. You see, dear, last evening Major Danforth invited Papa out for some amusement. Dear Danforth introduced himself and suggested cards, I suppose, and drink, and—well, I hope not women, but you know Papa. And if he's as bad as he used to be years ago the morning after, I wouldn't expect him here until five o'clock at the earliest. He will have to enquire for our lodgings as well as wake up, remember."

"How sweet of the major," said Leonora. "Don't you think him gallant and quite romantic? He was trying to spare you pain."

Billie shrugged. "I'm sure Danforth means well. But no gentleman would have done less."

Leonora bit back a sigh of exasperation. Billie was determined not to give credit where it was due. "Mr. Forrester was quite kind, too," Leonora said, partly to irritate her sister, but chiefly out of an irresistible desire to talk about the man. "He rescued me from Papa, and we had the first dance."

"And the second. Don't think I wasn't watching."

"How could you have been? You were busy dancing yourself, as I recall. And after you promised not to!"

The sisters glared at each other; then they burst out laughing. "Let's not quarrel," said Billie. "Perhaps I did dance, but Sir Hector was most attentive."

"People who insist on dressing in mourning don't dance, Billie. And Sir Hector was what he always is: a leering popinjay."

"But a wealthy one. Did I tell you my information's in on that dear man? He does have a house in Town, and my sources say four thousand a year."

Leonora looked severe. "You oughtn't to keep throwing yourself at that horrid man."

"*I* throw myself? I wasn't the one languishing in Forrester's arms for all the world to see. And he without two farthings to rub together. I was embarrassed for you, Leonora."

"A country dance cannot be called a romantic interlude," Leonora pointed out, "and while we're on the subject—"

But Billie declined to spar further. She interrupted with, "I don't know but what it wouldn't be more sensible for me to hold out for Lord Carlisle. Absurdly rich, and there wouldn't be long to wait—"

"Billie!"

A strained silence followed. Esmé chose this interesting moment to enter with the breakfast things, and as she spread the cloth and laid it with coffee, bread and butter, and cold ham, her long eyes all the while observing each sister in turn, Leonora wondered if the privations of the Peninsula, added to the strain of a less than perfect marriage, had completely turned Billie's head. Carlisle! Leonora saw in her mind the frail old man in his exquisite clothes, being carried into the room the last night but one by Forrester.

Esmé disappeared into Billie's bedroom for the morning chores, leaving the sisters alone.

"Lord Carlisle would be a delightful husband," said Billie in a low, determined voice. "Mind you, I don't know if he'd think of marriage, but it's worth a try. At least I wouldn't starve. Whereas you, Sister, have attached the interest of the one man in Cheltenham who is surely more interested in your dowry than anything else!''

"My dowry?''

"Yes, your dowry. Papa has provided very well for you, I'm sure. Why else would such an obviously poor man attach himself to a girl like you, a girl of good family? If he were honest, and half as principled as he pretends to be charming, he'd admit he wasn't good enough for you and leave you alone.''

Leonora paused to consider this logic. "But—''

"And what did Forrester do last night, immediately, but start making up to Papa?'' Billie cut a slice of ham and bit into it, looking at Leonora with pity.

"Forrester was only trying to help me escape Papa,'' protested Leonora. "He couldn't manage that by insulting him.''

"He's a rake and an adventurer,'' said Billie. "You've lived a sheltered life, my dear, but I've been knocking about the world for, er, thirty years now.''

"Thirty-five,'' muttered Leonora.

"And I've learned a few things along the way. Such as how to recognize a man who isn't what he pretends to be.''

Leonora was putting together another retort when there came a banging at the door.

"Papa!'' Billie whispered, her eyes suddenly wide.

"Leonora!'' that very gentleman's voice bellowed through the portal.

"What shall we do?'' Leonora whispered back. "Make believe we're not here?''

"What will the landlady say? Or the neighbours?'' fretted Billie, still speaking softly.

The pounding and yelling continued. Esmé appeared at the door of Billie's bedroom, a pillow in her hands. She tossed it aside and strode to the door, a small, determined figure.

"Esmé! No!" cried both sisters. But the maid opened the door.

Sir John burst into the room, saw his daughters, and made as if to push past the diminutive servant.

Esmé lifted her skirt. A hand clapped to her garter.

What happened next was uncertain, but within ten seconds Sir John Clare was backed against the door with a small, sharp knife pricking at his throat.

"The *señora* not like this one," said Esmé into the shocked silence. She flashed a grin. "I finish him, madam?"

"Heavens, no. That's my father. But do keep watch on him."

Leonora stared. She would never have thought to see Billie looking so indifferent, so calm, at a scene such as this.

Billie caught her sister's eye. "There was a little more to life in the Peninsula than not enough food and those ghastly battles."

Leonora nodded, unable to speak.

Sir John, once the knife had retreated a distance from his throat, began to bluster. "Good God, Leonora, get your things. Never heard of such a show. Your own father, Wilhelmina!"

"Why, Papa," said Billie. "Those are the first words you've spoken to me in years. Perhaps I ought to open some champagne."

"Champagne, indeed! Corrupting a young girl," grumbled Sir John, his tone uneven as the dangerous Esmé rounded on him again with her weapon.

"I am no longer a young girl, Papa," said Leonora. "Nor am I under any obligation to go home with you until you...until Mrs. Rose..."

"I'll cut you off without a penny!" thundered Sir John.

"Papa," Billie spoke up, "you will leave this house now. If you'll take my advice, you'll be careful what you say. One never knows when my maid might take matters into her own hands. A violent people, these Spanish."

"*Violencia?*" Esmé's eyes lit up, and she brandished her knife. "*A sus órdenes, Señora.*"

"She would be glad to do you an injury at my instructions, Papa," translated Billie.

"A hanging offence! You'd not risk it, even if she is only a Spanish gel. A bluff and nothing more," Sir John said. Now that the shock of his entrance was over, his daughters could see the bags under his eyes, the bleariness of his countenance. Major Danforth must have given him a fine tour of the seamier side of the town.

"Papa," Leonora said, "Billie has asked you to go. Perhaps you had better, before we all say things we'll regret. Tell me where you're staying. I'll send over my remedy for what ails you."

Sir John shuddered. Leonora's remedy, involving white mustard and a raw egg among other noxious ingredients, was a far cry from the small beer he favoured to help him over the blue devils. "Trying to kill me, too, are ye? Ten to one you'd send it by that Spanish virago." He indicated Esmé, who still stood near him, running the knife in and out between her fingers. The girl flashed him a wicked grin.

"I may be tempted to do precisely that, Papa, if you don't leave at once," said Billie.

"Trollop," said Sir John succinctly.

Leonora gasped, but Billie merely looked annoyed.

"It serves me right for wearing this tartish robe," she said. "Well, Papa? You may leave now. I'll hope to hear that you've gone home to Greenhill."

"You can't dictate to me, girl. Now I'm here, I'll stay as long as I choose."

A short silence fell. Then Billie turned to speak to Leonora. "Perhaps we can turn this situation to account, dear. Our father paying us a morning call, and staying in Cheltenham to bear us company. I haven't felt so respectable in years. Ever since he disowned me."

"Why, Billie," Leonora responded, feeling very proud of her sister, "how wise you are."

"Lend countenance to this unnatural child? That I'll never do," said Sir John with a careless wave at Billie, dashing Leonora's momentary hopes that the breach of years could be healed in an instant.

"You already have," Billie stated. Her eyes were beginning to sparkle. "I never thought I'd say this, but thank you, Papa."

Sir John visibly fumed. Leonora, observing him, thought she understood him. He had come raging to Cheltenham, probably desperate for Leonora to take over the reins of the household (for Mrs. Rose, Leonora had reason to know, was no manager except, evidently, of men) only to find that his lifelong weapons of intimidation and blustering were no longer effective. She suspected that he wanted her to come back home not only to keep the house, but because he missed her, and that if he did stay on in Cheltenham it would be to be near his daughters.

"We are glad to see you here, Papa," she said.

This was too much for Sir John. He had stormed into the lodging intent upon insulting one daughter and dragging the other back to Wiltshire, but they were not having any of it. "I wash my hands of you both," he muttered.

Jamming his hat, which had never left his head, more firmly onto his grizzled pate, he uttered a final curse and left the lodging, slamming the door behind him.

Esmé, her eyes snapping with enjoyment, was more animated in the aftermath of her heroics than Leonora had ever seen her. With a saucy curtsy she returned to the bedroom and her interrupted task.

Billie took another slice of bread-and-butter.

"Does Esmé always have a knife by her?" asked Leonora hesitantly.

Billie gave a wry smile. "I ought to have mentioned to you before, Leonora, that she's usually armed. So am I, come to think on it."

"You're joking."

"Oh, no." And Billie stood up, opened her robe, and revealed the tiny knife tucked into her ribbon garter. "I never notice it, but it puts my mind at rest. The stiletto is quite à la mode in Spain."

Leonora had the unsettling sensation of having sat down to breakfast with a sister who had changed into a stranger before her eyes. It was on the tip of her tongue to ask Billie whether she had ever used the knife, but she decided she would really rather not know.

"You would be wasted on Lord Carlisle or Sir Hector," was all she said, with a look of admiration.

Billie dimpled and touched her hair. "That's as may be. Do you know, dear, if I were you I would send round your blue-devil concoction to Papa. Ten to one he's putting up at the Plough. Can you make it extra nasty?"

"You are an evil woman," said Leonora. "Remind me never to get really cross with you. When I think that I've spent the morning arguing with a lady who was concealing a weapon! It makes me quite faint."

"Nothing has ever made you faint, Leonora," said Billie. "You and I are alike in that way. Perhaps you'll need your pluck some day. I've made use of mine from time to time." She sighed. "Ten years ago, or even five, I would have turned into a watering pot at Papa's words this morning. But now—well, I simply know that I can't take the trouble to do so."

The remainder of breakfast passed in peace, without mention of Forrester, Sir Hector Markham or any other gentleman who might have caused the ladies to disagree.

CHAPTER NINE

LEONORA and Portia Pickering stood in a corner of Lady Markham's drawing-room, putting their heads together over a copy of *Wild Oats*. Portia was petrified. On this, the second day of rehearsals, the players were not only to read their parts, they were to walk through, and Portia was certain she would trip or worse if made to read and move about at the same time.

Leonora did her best to reassure her young friend, but in truth she was as frightened as anyone in the room. It wasn't so much fear of appearing foolish as of Lady Markham, whose disapproval was awful to behold.

Billie, to Leonora's disgust, had clamped on to Sir Hector and was simpering under his eye like a lovesick schoolgirl. Having glimpsed the fiery military widow of the day before, a brave woman who kept her head in the most outrageous of situations, Leonora couldn't like seeing her sister as the cooing ninny she affected before Sir Hector.

The rest of the party was dispersed about the elegant salon, engaging in social chatter as they waited for Lady Markham.

"Oh! Do look," Portia whispered into Leonora's ear. "Mama will be so happy to hear of this." She gave a nervous giggle. "I wish I could be."

Leonora glanced in the direction Portia was indicating and saw Lord Stone striding towards them. A bit more energy than usual was apparent in his step. His long face betrayed a shyness which belied—or perhaps reinforced—the extravagance of his costume. The baron bowed over Leonora's hand and then Portia's. A wave of lank hair fell over his forehead and brushed each fair hand in turn.

"Thought I'd join you ladies," he said. "Not clever, you know. I could do with a bit of practice on this theatrical thing."

"We're all about to have that whether we will or no," said Leonora. "Tell me, my lord, have you acted before? Your mother is such an enthusiast."

"Stepmother," said Stone quickly. "Not mother. No, I never trod the boards m'self. Nor did Mama." He stared at them in dismay.

Leonora had the sudden feeling that he was afraid they had accused his mother of some vulgarity. She knew not how to repair the impression, but she had certainly meant nothing of the sort.

"Her ladyship seemed so knowledgeable," ventured Portia.

"Yes. She has such definite ideas on what she wants. That's all we wished to say," Leonora added.

"Knowledgeable? Mama? Couldn't be. If she ain't ever acted—and she ain't—she can't very well know about it. Ah, I have it! She's seen plays. Seen 'em and knows what she likes."

"To be sure," murmured Leonora.

"Well, I must say how d'ye do to those chaps over there," said Stone. He walked off too quickly, Leonora thought, almost as if he wished to get away from them, whereas he had approached them with such eagerness.

"What an odd young man," she said. "Do you suppose we said something to offend him?"

"Oh, we couldn't have, Leonora," returned Portia. "He isn't very striking, is he? My mother thinks he'd be so perfect for me. But I'd hoped—"

Leonora squeezed the young lady's shoulders. "Keep hoping, dear. You're only seventeen, and Lord Stone doesn't . . . he must have very good qualities, but . . ."

"But," agreed Portia, and that seemed to be all there was to say. "Oh, my goodness! Here comes your beau. Such a handsome man. Might I be introduced today, do you think? Not that he would ever look at me when you're in the room, dear Leonora. You're so lovely, and I'm such a . . ." She hesitated.

Leonora said kindly, but in perfect truth, "Such a very pretty girl," and then broke out into a smile. What in the world was Forrester doing here, walking about the room as though he belonged in it?

Murmurs followed the handsome but shabby gentleman. Billie was frowning and whispering something to Sir Hector. Luckily, some of the other players seemed to have met Forrester, and many hailed him with friendliness.

Leonora also greeted him happily and introduced him to the wide-eyed Miss Pickering. That young miss dimpled, blushed, and murmured something unintelligible.

"What are you doing here, sir?" Leonora then asked. "I thought you met the Markhams only the other night."

"Well, Miss Clare, I will tell you." He gave Leonora a glance so tender that little Miss Pickering sighed in envy. "I was most eager to join this happy group, so when I met her ladyship again in the High Street yesterday I regaled her with tales of my expertise as a prompter. Overcame her with my charm, in fact. She admitted she might hesitate to let me join the project if she had daughters, for I appear to be a dangerous rogue, says she. But since all of you young ladies are provided with chaperons, she consented to have me." He winked.

"I'm all admiration," said Leonora. "I needn't warn you that my sister won't be pleased to see you here. She'll probably say something unmannerly."

"I'm used to it, and as I understand her point of view, I cannot take offence."

"You understand?" Leonora, who had so often congratulated herself on her lack of tendency to blush, turned scarlet.

Forrester grinned. "If I had a pretty sister, I wouldn't trust a chance-met man of mystery either."

Miss Pickering couldn't suppress another sigh at this well-turned compliment.

Leonora looked into Forrester's eyes. What honest brown eyes they were—or seemed to be. "Why are you a man of mystery, sir? Major Danforth seems to be your only acquaintance, and he knows nothing about you. He wasn't even sure of your name, as I recall. Isn't it always better to be candid with Society?"

"But of course. A sound principle to which I fully subscribe."

Before Leonora could find the words for another question, Lady Markham entered the room and clapped her hands to get the group's attention. "My men have just finished putting the theatre together. Such a cunning job." She noticed the smiling Forrester and hailed him. "Here's our new prompter. Heavens, but you look familiar, young man, especially from across a room. Well, come along. Ladies! Gentlemen!"

All the players-to-be were quick to answer their marching orders. They trooped through the front hall and into the dining room, which was situated at the back of the house.

Leonora had not seen the room in its character of a dining parlour, but she was willing to believe that it had been such, and recently. The force of Lady Markham's personality had swept through it to good effect. Now the room looked as if it had been conceived as a theatre.

A stage was built along one side of the room, complete with green baize curtain. Chairs, no doubt belonging to the exiled dining-table, stood ranged in rows before the wooden proscenium. Leonora looked at the chairs and shuddered, realizing fully for the first time that she was to perform—*perform*—before an audience of strangers.

"Capital arrangement, my lady," cried one gentleman. There was a pause in the day's business as everyone else also congratulated Lady Markham on her magnificent little theatre.

"A rather snug little thing, ain't it?" she said. "And the door at the rear of the stage, which will be covered by the flats, leads to the library. We'll use it for our Green Room."

"Oh, ma'am," said Lady Cecilia, "it will be such a shame to take it down when we're finished."

"We've a fair amount of work to do before that day comes," Lady Markham assured the lady. She fumbled among the wealth of golden chains on her bosom and came up with her eyeglass. "Now, places, everyone. Mr. Boyles, Ensign Derwent: on stage! Mr. Hampton and Miss Clare, be ready to go on. Look sharp, everyone!"

Lady Markham established herself in a third row seat and rattled her manuscript in a businesslike manner. Those cast members who had not been called onstage mingled about in varying states of nervousness. Two footmen circled the room, offering trays of refreshment to the guests, but other than that one trapping of wealth there was no sign that this was anything other than a bona fide rehearsal.

Leonora was told to go up onto the stage and into the wings and stand with Mr. Forrester in a place handy for her entrance.

"We must begin as we mean to go on," said Lady Markham.

Leonora was quick to obey such a pleasant instruction. Forrester was giving his manuscript copy his every attention, for he could be clearly seen by her ladyship. Still he had a special, private smile for Leonora.

Leonora returned his smile even though Lady Markham was watching. Billie she didn't worry about, for Mrs. Smithers was still talking with Sir Hector.

Very soon Mr. Boyles and Ensign Derwent had finished their short tête-à-tête; Mr. Hampton went on; then it was Leonora's turn. Remembering Lady Markham's compliment about her "carrying" voice, Leonora didn't dare to mumble. She nearly shouted.

"Very good, Miss Clare," interrupted Lady Markham, her own voice ringing with approval.

Leonora hoped that Lady Markham's approval was only for her vocal capabilities. Her ladyship was rumoured to be quite selective when it came to the question of a mate for her stepson. It couldn't be that she approved of Leonora. Could it? Leonora struggled to keep her mind on her lines, worrying.

Lord Stone was doubtless under the thumb of his stepmother. If Lady Markham did, for whatever reason, approve of Leonora as a match, Leonora would be faced with hurting that rather pitiful young baron.

Her face was downcast as she returned to the wings, and, not so incidentally, the side of Mr. Forrester. He whispered some compliment to her, and she was immediately cheered. They were able to exchange the occasional word as other players came and went, and Lady Markham called out instructions, criticisms, and the rare compliment.

"She seems so professional," murmured Leonora to Forrester. "I could almost fancy myself at Drury Lane."

"Hmm. Professional. But she, the widow of a baron and a baronet, could hardly have such experience?"

"Her stepson says not. He's probably mistaken, though, and her ladyship has acted at theatrical house parties."

"Yes, the lady was undoubtedly a Juliet to some creaking peer's Romeo," said Forrester, and Leonora had to stifle a giggle.

When the performers were allowed a short break after the third act, Portia hurried up to Leonora's side. "I know I shall die of this," cried the girl. "Did you hear what she said to me?"

In the incident under discussion Lady Markham had risen in her chair to call Miss Pickering a "mealy-mouthed schoolroom chit." This being very close to the truth, it had hurt the more.

"I shall quit," continued Portia stoutly. "Mama will never make me come back when she knows the hardships I'm facing."

Forrester came up behind the ladies in time to hear this. "Buck up, Miss Pickering," he said. "No need to fly into the boughs. Lady Markham has a brusque way about her, but it doesn't signify. She just called me a 'devil of an insolent puppy.'"

"She did?" Portia gazed at him in wonder.

"Yes, because I suggested that she might be giving the wrong advice to Mr. Boyles in his Sir George character."

"You gave advice to Lady Markham?" gasped Leonora.

"Well, ma'am, you have told me before that I'm too bold. Or was it your sister who said that?"

"Doubtless both of us."

"In any case, Miss Pickering, consider yourself one of the group and be a sport about the matter," urged Forrester.

"Oh, sir! If you think it would be best . . ."

"I do. Now, if you will excuse me, ma'am, I'd like to have a private word with Miss Clare before our lady general has us muster for Act Four."

Portia's eyes widened, and she had a conspiratorial nod for Leonora before she obediently walked away to the place at the edge of operations where her maid was sitting.

"Well, sir?" Leonora tried to look severe. "We shouldn't exchange so much as a syllable in even this much privacy."

"Miss Clare, I simply wanted to tell you why I secured this post as prompter. Or would you care to guess?"

Leonora brightened. His reasons might be a clue to his ambiguous position in Society. She dared one facetious guess. "An invalid's way of passing the time while taking the waters?"

Forrester laughed. "You still don't believe in my complaint. I must be flattered that you think I look healthy. Well, ma'am, I want to be honest with you, for you admire such behaviour. Here it is, then: I wormed my way into this house solely to be in your company. What can a fellow do who is barred from a lady's home? I can't carry Lord Carlisle up your sister's stairs every time I wish to see you."

"I think you're being bold again," said Leonora softly, sensible of a great fluttering in the region of her bosom.

"Faint heart never won fair lady," responded Forrester. "Do you blame me very much?"

Leonora cast down her eyes. "You must know what is best for you to do sir. I hope you enjoy the play, at least, if my company becomes burdensome."

She was becoming dangerously attracted to this man. Her sister's disapproval aside, how could Leonora consider Forrester a serious suitor? She knew nothing of his family or his pursuits—and he wasn't telling.

Perhaps this was one of those watering-place flirtations she had heard about; he would trifle with her, they would dance together and banter whenever they met, until their respective visits were over. There was nothing wrong in that. Leonora felt a little pang, though, wondering how quickly Forrester would forget her when he moved on to the next place, the next young lady.

"Thoughtful, ma'am? I hope I haven't depressed you with my heavy-handed attentions," said her companion.

"Oh, no, sir. We were talking of...the play. How do you like it?" Leonora determined to keep the conversation, and all subsequent conversations with him, on an innocuous level. Talking about his attraction to her was delightful, but where could such words lead? Only to a confession of her attraction to him, which she must not allow.

"O'Keeffe is a brilliant writer, and the comedy is a delight," was Forrester's instant answer. "My favourite sort of play, these mixed-up plots where the whole outcome rests on a case of mistaken identity."

"Not much like real life," Leonora said. "Or—" Suddenly she thought of her sister, hiding a multitude of strengths under that silly public exterior. "Perhaps there are many people who aren't quite what they seem."

He laughed. "You mean to be severe upon me, ma'am."

She decided to confide her earlier thoughts about Billie. "You must know best about your own case, sir. Actually, I was thinking of my sister. She acts such a cake when she's with the gentlemen. She's really a different person at home."

"I suppose many of us could say that."

"But not I," said Leonora firmly.

"Oh, no, ma'am, not you. Your character is as clear as day, and as easy to interpret."

Leonora frowned; this didn't sound like a compliment. Before she could make any answer, the voice of Lady Markham was heard, calling the players back to their duty.

"Miss Clare. Discovered on stage, if you'll recall?" her ladyship shouted across the room.

"And so ends our conversation. I see your sister looking quite relieved," said Forrester. "I salute you, my honest lady. I shall be right behind you, prompting book at the ready."

Leonora hurried to her task, wondering if a more infuriating, more delightful gentleman had ever walked the earth.

CHAPTER TEN

THE SUMMER ORGANIZED itself into neat patterns, unlike the first easygoing days of Leonora's visit to the spa. She no longer had time to stroll the lanes and byways in search of plants. Now she seemed always to be at Lady Markham's disposal, as the date set for the performance drew ever nearer.

Leonora did not discover in herself a great facility or talent for acting. She suspected she was passable and no more, though her voice was an undeniable asset. Billie continued to glory in the role of Leonora's chaperon at the rehearsals, casting her hook ever deeper into Sir Hector, or so she thought. For Leonora, the high point of these gatherings was the constant presence of Forrester. Though his talents as prompter were rarely needed in her case, he always had a smile and a flirtatious word for her.

As for Sir John Clare, a silent truce had been declared between him and his daughters. He had indeed decided to stay on in Cheltenham. Race week was his interest, he told Leonora when they met in the High Street one day. He'd sent down to Wiltshire for Gentleman's Fancy, his most promising mare, and would run her for the first time on Cleeve Downs.

Leonora and Billie were both relieved that Papa was being reasonable. He was staying at the Plough, out of their way, and by his very presence he lent a certain countenance to their little household. Leonora was rather indignant that the seeming approval of such a character as Papa could aid her sister's reputation, but so it appeared to be. Society was an incredible maze of falsities, Leonora thought resentfully.

One day a strange rumour reached Leonora's ears. She heard that Sir John often walked down to the Old Well of a morning, arm in arm with Lady Markham.

Leonora was sceptical, knowing that Papa hated mineral waters as much as he hated getting up in the morning. Furthermore, he and Lady Markham, when they'd met at the first assembly, had seemed antagonistic, and Leonora had not seen them together since.

The very morning after she heard the story happened to be a rare free day due to some plans of Lady Markham's. Leonora gave up the walk she had long anticipated, to Marle Hill at the north, and instead went the short distance from Billie's lodgings to the Well Walk. The avenue of tall elms was quite pleasant, and the rustic bridge over the River Chelt must charm, but Leonora, who loved the country lanes, would not have chosen such a crowded place if she had not had an ulterior motive. Elderly ladies and gentlemen were being wheeled towards the Pump Room in their Bath chairs; the less infirm or merely sociable strolled in their finest summer costumes in the same direction. The Well Walk was the chief promenade of the town, and Leonora was finding that Society on parade was a thing she preferred in small doses. Trying to appear casual, she started down the broad walk in the midst of the crowd, glancing about for Papa.

She had made one promenade to the Pump Room, looked in, and was halfway back to St. Mary's church, where the walk began, when she saw them.

She quickly stepped into the shade of an elm tree. There, strolling along with every appearance of friendliness, were

Papa and Lady Markham. Her ladyship, in an enormous leghorn bonnet decked with five colours of plumes, was clinging to Sir John's brawny arm while he leant down to tell her something.

"They can't like each other," Leonora said aloud.

"And why not? Stranger matches have been made. Dear Miss Clare, why are you hiding your beauty in the shadows? Let's join your esteemed parent and your even more esteemed director."

Leonora, looking up into Forrester's laughing face, realized that she had not only come to the Well Walk to look for Papa. In the back of her mind had been the notion that Forrester, if he really took the waters, might be here, too.

"Do you make a habit of lurking in shadows, sir?"

"No. But I might as well warn you, since you've discovered those two have been forming a friendship, that Lady Markham would be a dashed uncomfortable stepmama."

"Why, how would you know what sort of stepmama she would be sir? And certainly it can't have gone that far." She couldn't believe that Papa, whose taste in females ran to the voluptuous and youthful, would have a serious interest in the forceful and fiftyish Lady Markham.

Forrester ignored Leonora's first question. "Your father's of a rank with Lady Markham's last husband, if not her first, and it seems to me I see a predatory look in her eye these days. And she's so approving of you. Perhaps you are a prospective daughter in more ways than one."

"I should be quite relieved to think that Lady Markham wants me to be her stepdaughter through Papa instead of through Lord Stone."

"Then you wouldn't consider the baron? You would snap your fingers at the greatest catch of the Season?"

She looked at him sharply. "It's no business of yours, sir, but no, I would not consider his lordship." About to add, "Who would?" she checked herself out of belated delicacy and consideration for the absent young man.

"But perhaps your feelings *are* my business," said Forrester.

Leonora was too pleased by this comment to offer a retort. She stood gazing at him with a mixture of embarrassment and wonder. He, she noticed through her haze, was looking at her most tenderly.

Finally he broke the spell. "Shall we follow the love-birds?" he said briskly, and held out his arm.

Leonora found that the thought of walking anywhere with Forrester held great appeal, and she was happy enough to return to the business which had brought her out. They began a rather quick promenade in the direction of the Pump Room, trying to come up with the elder pair. Finally, at the door of the establishment, Forrester touched Sir John on the arm.

"Eh?" The baronet turned round. "What, you here, Leonora? And with this jackanapes? Where's your maid?"

"My sister's maid is busy about the house," answered Leonora. "How do you do, Lady Markham?"

Her ladyship's face changed colour under her rouge. "Miss Clare. Your father and I met by chance, and as we both take two glasses from the pump each day, we decided to walk together."

"No need to explain, my lady," said Leonora, daring to smile slyly. "Papa is capable of being most charming when he wishes."

"Er, quite so," blustered Sir John. He looked exactly like a small boy caught out in mischief. "You out for a walk, Leonora? I'd hate to keep you."

"Oh, I have plenty of time," said Leonora. "Do you, Mr. Forrester? We met by chance, Papa," she added.

"By chance," echoed Mr. Forrester with an air of great propriety. "I have nothing but time, and I was going in to take my daily glass, too. If Miss Clare will indulge us..."

"I've been meaning to try some of the local waters," Leonora said. It was true; she had wished to analyse the various springs of Cheltenham while she was in the town, the object being a sort of essay on their probable properties for her receipt book of medical and cosmetic remedies.

"Ah, I forget Miss Clare would have a professional interest. The waters can do as much good as herbs, can they not, ma'am?"

"That's why I'd like to try them; I don't know," said Leonora. The main object, which she could not state, was to keep Papa and Lady Markham under her eye for as long as possible to judge the nature of their attachment.

She took her father's arm and proceeded into the Pump Room. Behind her she could hear Lady Markham informing Forrester, "I have it, young man. I've been cudgeling my brain trying to think where I've seen you. You were at Bath two winters ago with your old auntie, Lady Prendergast. That's it!"

"Well..." Forrester hesitated, and Leonora wondered if someone had at last broken the gentleman's iron reserve on the subject of his past. To her disappointment, he answered with his customary satire. "I can't really say, my lady. I don't keep such track of my movements that I can deny being in Bath in '11, but what does concern me about your theory is that I can't remember an Aunt Prendergast. Unfortunate, but there it is."

"Humph," sniffed Lady Markham.

"What do you mean by distinguishing Lady Markham, sir?" Leonora asked in a low voice, drawing her father to one side as the others approached the pump and the pump woman gave them their glasses.

Sir John leaned close. "The old bird is warm as they come. And—" He hesitated and looked a bit puzzled, as if thinking over his reasoning for the first time. "We appear to suit. Odd, ain't it?"

Leonora looked at him in amazement. "Then your intentions are serious?"

"Might be," Sir John said.

Leonora reflected that a healthy respect for "the ready" had always governed her father's actions; had indeed been behind his rejection of Billie. Still, the thought of Papa marrying again, for whatever reason, was a strange one. She was glad that Lady Markham was so evidently a lady who could take care of herself.

The iron-laden waters of the Old Well were as bitter as Leonora had thought they would be, and she struggled to drink her glass without choking while the others took theirs.

Forrester winked at Leonora as he gamely drained his glass without a suggestion of discomfort. "A dish of tea in the Long Room wouldn't come amiss, would it? Lady Markham, will you lend your countenance to Miss Clare? Sir John, I know you'll be delighted at the opportunity for these two ladies to become better acquainted."

Sir John coughed into his second glass of water, but since Lady Markham looked interested he could not refuse.

When they were seated in the pleasant, pilastered room with tea and buttered rolls before them, Mr. Forrester said, "Lady Markham, I've heard a sad story going about regarding your first husband's sons...if it would not overly distress you to talk about it.''

Leonora couldn't help staring. This was a strange subject for Forrester to open. She didn't know him well, but he didn't seem the sort either to repeat gossip or to be interested in its source.

Lady Markham sat up straighter in her chair at his words, her eyes softening as she looked off into the distance, presumably recollecting the days when she had been Lady Stone. "You must have heard of the elder boy's sad death. The poor, dear young man." She sighed. "Naturally, not having been blessed with children of my own, Lord Stone's were as dear to me as if I'd borne them. The heir left us at the age of twelve. Joined up as a drummer, of all things, for the boy was mad to fight the French. Inconvenient behaviour in an heir, my dear Lord Stone used to say. He found the lad after a good deal of time, trouble, and government influence, and sent him off to school, and there young Dickon stayed until he was old enough to be bought a pair of colours. He had to have his way, and Lord Stone gave in. Well, years went by, and his father hardly saw him. Nor did I, for my health has been plaguing me for years, Mr. Forrester, and I was always off at some spa or other when Dickon was home on his rare visits."

"How it must have comforted you both to have your other stepson at home with you—the present Lord Stone," said Leonora when Lady Markham paused for breath. She did not find this tale overly interesting and was wondering even more why Forrester had bothered to bring it up. Being such a polite and socially adept young man, he had perhaps sensed the lady's pleasure in dwelling on a family tragedy.

"Ah, it's true." Lady Markham dabbed at one eye with a handkerchief. "Mighty dangerous to have the head of a family in the army. Only last year, many years after my first husband's death, we had word his elder son had been killed at Badajoz. And so sweet Poynton, the Lord Stone you've met, had the title thrust upon him."

"Thrust," murmured Forrester, sipping his tea. "He does indeed, madam, appear to be a young man who is surprised to find a title sitting on his shoulders."

"Would you say so, sir?" Lady Markham's brow darkened. "Lord Stone is a most noble young man, I will have you know."

"Oh, I don't dispute that, my lady," Forrester assured her. "I only meant to say that he perhaps expected to live a quieter life than he does presently. He has become such an ornament to Society, and so quickly."

Lady Markham appeared to be much mollified by this assessment of her stepson.

"What a sad story, ma'am, about the military Lord Stone," Leonora felt compelled to say, after a few minutes had passed with no further reaction from the gentlemen than Forrester's thoughtful silence and Sir John's yawns. "My sister has told me of the many who died at Badajoz."

Lady Markham nodded. "Sad it was indeed. A young man cut down in the flower of his youth! And the vexing thing was, Miss Clare, that we had to go to some trouble to prove my stepson's claim to the title. The Stones always lived retired in the country, don't you know. And it happened that somehow a rumour had got about that dear Poynton had died in infancy! Never disproved, for we didn't know it existed. We got the claim settled right enough with my testimony. For though by that time I was the widow of Sir Tristram Markham—who didn't last long, more's the pity—I still have the greatest of affection for the only stepson I have left. Everyone had to admit at last that Lord Stone was very much alive.''

Not so very *alive,* was Leonora's unworthy thought as she pondered the listless ways of the young baron.

Leonora's eyes met Forrester's, and she was shocked to see the calculating look on his face. His eyes focussed on her as she watched, and the typical, cheerful smile was at once back in place.

"Well, my lady, a touching tale, that," said Forrester in brisk tones. "Thank you for telling it. You ought to know, madam, that there is still a rumour going about that the second son really did die in infancy with the late Lady Stone, which would make your stepson an imposter. Shameful, isn't it, what people will say."

"People are mostly ignorant," sniffed Lady Markham, looking not at all alarmed.

"A pithy observation, dear lady," put in Sir John. Leonora realized, with a start, that this was Papa's version of fashionable banter. Could he really be set on Lady Markham? Leonora could imagine some pragmatic discussion of mutual finances. Papa wasn't handsome or charming, but a woman of Lady Markham's age, if she desired to marry again, couldn't quibble over the details. He was well off, and that might suffice in the end. He had said they suited. Did they truly?

"Well," said Lady Markham, "here comes my brother. Sir Hector!"

Leonora bit back a sigh as Sir Hector Markham, side-whiskers bristling, approached their table. He gave Leonora the usual raking glance which she was convinced he offered every female under the age of fifty. Forrester saw this and looked in evident disapproval at the baronet, which made Leonora feel as pleasantly protected as though Forrester had called Sir Hector out for taking liberties.

Sir Hector, noting the young man's expression, looked in like disdain at Forrester. After brief greetings to the company (pointedly excluding Mr. Forrester, whom he cut) he sat down without being asked and proceeded to regale the group with talk of the play's progress. His small part of Farmer Gammon suited him down to the ground. Even Miss Pickering was coming on in her role of the farmer's daughter. And, naturally, Miss Clare was perfection in her part.

"Her voice is well enough," said Lady Markham.

Leonora was amused at Sir Hector's pleasure in his role as the mean-spirited farmer. Remembering his performance in rehearsals, she wondered if his untutored brilliance could come from his sympathy with such a nasty character.

She jolted herself out of this mental wandering when she heard Lady Markham tell Sir John the date of the performance.

"What? Why, that's the day Gentleman's Fancy's to run," exclaimed Sir John. "Had to set it for Race Week, did you?" He looked disgruntled. If he was dangling after Lady Markham, he must attend the play. And Papa's preference in post-race activities, Leonora had reason to know, didn't run to respectable Society parties.

"My dear Sir John," said Lady Markham, "has it not occurred to you what a pleasant diversion these theatricals will be to my guests after a day spent watching such a deadly dull thing as the antics of some restive animals?"

Sir John's mouth gaped, and he visibly girded his loins for a stirring argument. Soon he and the lady were embroiled in a spirited quarrel over the relative amusement value of equine or human actors, turf or stage.

Leonora, exchanging a laughing glance with Mr. Forrester, wondered if a match between her father and Lady Markham might not, after all, be a good thing.

CHAPTER ELEVEN

"I SHALL NEVER BELIEVE IT," declared Billie. "Papa and Lady Markham? Absurd. Danforth, have you heard any such talk?"

Major Danforth had arrived to escort the sister to the theatre and stood, hat in hand, looking bemused. He started when Billie put the question to him.

"Can't say," was his rejoinder. "They've been seen together, ma'am, but—well, what can anyone say? They ain't of an age to cause a scandal, are they?"

"I wish someone would tell that to Papa," said Leonora, thinking of the cook at Greenhill.

"Perhaps Lady Markham will," suggested the major.

"Enough about Papa," Billie put in. "Major, what do you think? Is this gown too quiet?"

Billie had altered a lavender gown of Leonora's to fit herself. It was the most subdued costume Leonora had seen her sister wear. Leonora had made the mistake of telling Billie this, thinking it would be a compliment.

Major Danforth gave his love a thorough inspection. "By George, you're a lovely sight," he said.

"You always say that," said Billie petulantly. "The dress, Danforth—the dress!"

"A most fetching thing. New, too, ain't it? Looks in the style of what's been showing up on the visitors from London."

Billie was not to be cajoled. "Are you saying that my other gowns—"

"Sister," Leonora admonished, "when you go fishing for compliments, you mustn't throw them back." This set the party laughing, and they were off down the stairs and into the major's hackney coach, speculating as they neared the theatre on whether Papa or Lady Markham would be in the audience tonight. Leonora's chief concern was whether she would see Forrester. She touched her gown of blue silk mull, wondering if Forrester would tell her that it turned her eyes to blue.

When the party alighted at the Theatre Royal in the High Street, Billie told Leonora to follow her to the cloakroom.

"I have a confession to make," whispered Billie when she had got her sister alone. "I asked Sir Hector to meet us here. Do you think Danforth will let him into his box?"

"Everyone knows the major has no fondness for Sir Hector," Leonora said. "And considering how Danforth feels about you, it isn't surprising. Oh, Sister, when will you leave off chasing unsuitable men and see what's in front of your eyes?"

Billie looked angry; then her expression softened a very little. Her pretty face, peeking from under a flattering mantilla, was earnest as she said, "It's impossible that I should think of the major. All feelings aside, Danforth is to go back to the Peninsula very soon. Would you have me go through that experience again?"

"Not if you have such an aversion," replied Leonora, "though you've told me time and again of the adventures you enjoyed there. But isn't a fondness for the man in question supposed to make all inconvenience worthwhile?"

"What a romantic you still are, Leonora. By your age my eyes had been opened by experience. There are times when fondness doesn't solve everything. In fact, it complicates matters. If I hadn't been fond of Smithers, he couldn't have hurt me. Do you see what I mean?''

"No, not if your present logic is to marry a man you detest and console yourself with his money."

"But, Leonora, what choice is left me?" Billie cried. She was nearly in tears by now, and several ladies in the room looked at her oddly. "I have my pension, and that's all," she went on in a softer vein, dabbing at her eyes and glancing round at the other ladies with a bright and artificial smile. "What can a widow of my age do but remarry? If Smithers had provided for me, I might very well stay a widow forever. It's like being a married woman without the troubles . . . except the financial ones."

Leonora was silent. She had to concede that marriage was the only path open to Billie. She suspected, too, that Danforth's similarity to Major Smithers—at least in occupation and means—frightened Billie for deeper reasons.

Would Major Danforth leave the army? That would never do, for he would then have nothing, instead of only his pay. And there was something else. Leonora had seen relatively little of Danforth, except in social settings, but she knew that he showed animation only when he talked about going back to the wars. He would not be Danforth if he changed his life for Billie.

It occurred to Leonora that she was wishing her sister would do what Danforth could not do without resigning an essential part of his being: change. And why did it seem no more than proper for a woman to surrender all her ideals?

Leonora was frowning over her own prejudices, wondering if Mary Wollstonecraft had the correct notions with the Rights of Woman, when Billie touched her on the sleeve and told her to hurry along. The play was about to begin.

While Leonora scrutinized the performance with the new interest of the budding actress, her companions had their own games. Sir Hector, as Billie had foretold, indeed joined the three, and Major Danforth proved that he was every inch the gentleman when he made the infuriating baronet welcome. Sir Hector devoted himself to Billie with an air of casual intimacy which sickened Leonora. The major seethed, growing redder in the face as the play progressed. When Leonora looked up from her fascinated perusal of the stage at the first interval, she found Danforth touching her arm.

"The others went out into the corridor," he said gruffly. "Do you care to, ma'am?"

"No, thank you. Major, don't be misled by the way my sister throws herself at Sir Hector. I'd dare swear he doesn't care a rush for her, but he's the sort of man who'll always flirt back."

Danforth scowled. "I know what Wilhelmina is thinking, or I'm fairly sure I do. She's in her safe harbour now, back in England, and she'll stay even if she has to build on sand."

"What a nautical turn of phrase for an army man," said Leonora with a smile, trying to lighten the moment. "Do you go back to your regiment soon, sir?"

The major started. "Yes. Why do you ask?"

"Because we'll miss you. She will miss you. I'm sure she doesn't realize how much."

Danforth snorted in mingled pleasure and embarrassment. "I don't mind telling you, Miss Leonora, a part of me says 'twould serve her right. If it takes my going away to make her realize…well, I'll come back again one day."

Leonora stopped herself one second before she blurted out that he couldn't be sure he'd come back. "Did you ever think of simply asking her to marry you?" she said instead.

"Dozens of times. I do it nearly every day, or used to." A little smile peeked from under the major's moustache. "It don't serve, you know. 'Have you sold out and come into a fortune?' she asked me the first couple of times, and so I stopped."

Leonora sighed. "Then Billie is cruel, for she knows you love her, and she makes use of you to run her errands and escort us. It's a shame, Major. And you, sir—" she hesitated, well aware that she was about to say something unkind, but determined in the name of honesty to do it "—you are a fool."

Danforth started. Never before had Miss Clare said a word in his disfavour.

"I ought not to have been so blunt," Leonora quickly added. "I only mean it's a shame to keep dangling after someone who doesn't deserve you."

"But look at it this way, ma'am," Danforth pointed out. "My leave is up next month. Off I'll go. And am I not to see her in the meantime? Intolerable."

What on Earth had Billie ever done to inspire such devotion? Leonora reached out a hand and patted the major's, which was curled tensely about the railing.

It was at this moment that Mr. Forrester entered the box. Leonora turned round and saw him. He stared at the seemingly tender scene; the smile which had bedecked his face disappeared as she watched.

A pair of strangely cold brown eyes met Leonora's. "I would never have expected duplicity from you, ma'am," said Forrester.

Leonora was so astonished that she absentmindedly left her hand on Danforth's for a telling moment. Then she realized what she was doing, and snatched her hand back to her lap.

"Really, Mr. Forrester," she answered him with icy dignity. "I know you're an Original. I've seen you enter rooms by putting your foot in at the door; but I never thought you'd burst into a box and make unfounded accusations."

Forrester's eyes blazed, and Leonora saw more anger in his face than she would have believed possible. Then, as suddenly as he had come, he was gone.

Leonora appealed to the major. "Sir, you must know what he thought. Will you go after him and say that you and I weren't—aren't—are like brother and sister?"

Danforth's ears had turned an interesting vermilion. "Looks fit to call me out," he said. "You know, ma'am, your sister don't approve of that young man. She's said time and again you're not to think of him."

"Oh, yes," said Leonora. "You were the person she was going to quiz on Forrester's background and prospects. I presume, since she hasn't changed her mind about him, that the report which came back was unfavourable?"

"I hadn't any information for your sister on the Forrester chap," said the major. He rose. "Well, I'll do my best, Miss Leonora. He'd have to be queer in his attic to believe I'd dally with you—or you with me." He excused himself and left the box.

Leonora remained alone. She didn't doubt that a few words from Major Danforth would set all right between her and Forrester. He had been jealous! His misunderstanding of the situation was a shame; still, a most unworthy thought ran through her mind. How gratifying it was that she had excited his feelings to that degree! And how she and Forrester would laugh over his misconception when next they met. Perhaps he would come back to the box tonight....

She looked out over the rows of spectators and stared at the stage curtain, trying to take her mind off Forrester. Immediately her thoughts turned to the growing dread which possessed her more and more often. In only a few weeks she would be standing behind her own curtain, the swathes of green baize in Lady Markham's dining parlour. How would she ever manage to act?

AT REHEARSAL NEXT DAY, Leonora found that Major Danforth's eloquence had failed to work the expected miracle. Mr. Forrester was still angry with her.

"You try my patience, Miss Clare," was the only aside he muttered to her all morning, rattling his prompt book fiercely.

This was bad enough; then at the rest periods, instead of seeking Leonora out, Forrester dangled at the side of Lady Cecilia Crawe and gave Miss Clare a wide berth indeed.

"Your swain has deserted you for safer ground?" murmured Sir Hector into Leonora's ear.

She jumped; she hadn't realized what a forlorn figure she must make, standing at centre stage in what must be a drooping pose. And she certainly hadn't heard Sir Hector sneak up behind her.

"I have no swains, sir," she said with what she hoped was a light smile. "Haven't you heard? I'm a confirmed spinster."

"I thought you were my future niece," said the baronet. "Or ought I to say stepniece? These family relationships do confuse one. My stepnephew Poynton is most attentive."

Leonora felt bound to point out that Lord Stone had fled the room in an agony of stage fright after his last scene. "He isn't exactly dancing attendance," she added. "And you shouldn't believe everything you hear, Sir Hector. I shall not marry your stepnephew."

"Hmm. Lord Stone is a catch, my dear. And you and I would be so closely related. That might make things quite convenient."

Leonora couldn't believe what she was hearing. Did this revolting man think he was irresistible to every woman on Earth? "I would certainly have my sister with me often wherever I set up my household," she said, in an attempt to dissuade him from such a provoking subject.

"Mrs. Smithers is a lovely woman, but I wasn't discussing her," said the baronet with a wink.

Leonora decided that her best course would be to continue to misunderstand his meaning. "Weren't you? This line of talk is pointless anyway, sir. I shan't be marrying Lord Stone."

"But if my sister-in-law wishes it, Miss Clare, you might find yourself in a difficult position."

Leonora sighed and looked the baronet straight in the eye. "Sir Hector, I'm already in a difficult position. Several difficult positions. And whatever I do or am made to do, I must remember one thing: to be true to myself. And that plan does not include marriage with your nephew."

"How very Shakespearean of you, young lady. May I make a wager with you? You'll come round. My nephew has a title and estate, and you can't be so unlike the rest of your family that you'll give up a chance to feather your nest."

Leonora gasped. "Excuse me, sir. I'm not so used to fashionable Society that I am prepared to take an insult to me and my family lightly." Turning on her heel, she walked away to the back of the stage and went through the connecting door to the library, turned Green Room.

Had the whole world gone mad? Leonora found the library empty and sat down in a leather armchair to think things over. Sir Hector was making up to two sisters at once. He evidently expected them both to dally with him. Leonora wondered if she should tell Billie of Sir Hector's sly overtures. Would such a talk have the desired effect of making Billie mistrust Sir Hector, or would she merely shrug, say men would be men, and count out his fortune on her fingers?

Leonora's thoughts next turned to Papa and Lady Markham. What if they did marry? Home might be unbearable with Lady Markham as her stepmama; the lady would take the household into an iron grip. On the bright side, Lady Markham would never want to bury herself in the country, and Leonora, as stepdaughter, would likely travel with her ladyship wherever she went. And—Leonora's smile broke out—Lady Markham would make short work of Papa's cook!

The door to the stage opened and Lord Stone came in. Leonora hailed him, not out of a desire for his company, but because she had a curiosity about the enigmatic young man which would never be solved as long as she kept to her normal programme of avoiding him. Seeing Miss Clare, the young baron hurried over and sat down opposite her in another library chair.

Lord Stone's idea of romance seemed to be to put on a rather mooning expression. At assemblies and during breaks in the rehearsals, he clung to Leonora's side like a burr. But he did nothing else; did not turn compliments nor even cast glances of much significance. Leonora couldn't tell if he really admired her or merely had had instructions from his stepmother to begin a courtship.

It really made no matter; Leonora wished she could shake him off, but he wasn't much trouble when he was near. How, she had often asked herself, could the attentions of such a cipher do a young lady such social good as everyone assured her? As the apparent chosen bride of Lord Stone, she had seen her status rising of late. And how unfairly! She would never marry him.

"I was looking for you, ma'am." Stone indicated the manuscript clutched in his hands. "Thought I saw you come in here. This play is the very devil of a thing, ain't it? Can't even sleep nights anymore for worrying. Shall we do that scene Mama was yelling about earlier?"

"Of course I'll practise with you, sir," said Leonora, struck by the honest note of fright in his voice as he discussed the play. She could certainly understand his fears, for she was beset by many herself. "I should fetch my sister," she added, for it had just occurred to her what a compromising situation this was. Not that the mild Lord Stone would try to take liberties; but if they were found alone together in a closed room he might be forced to offer for her, and her refusal, coming before the play was presented, would make things most uncomfortable.

"Oh, don't do that, ma'am. I have Forrester coming in to help us," said Lord Stone with a shy grin.

Leonora understood that the young man might find Billie's gushing uncomfortable, but she felt the hair at the back of her neck prickle at the mention of Forrester. "All the more reason to get my sister," she said with a smile, standing up. "One lady and two gentlemen alone together! It would never do."

She hurried to the door, half intending not to come back to the gentlemen with or without her sister, when Forrester entered. "Ah, there you are, Miss Clare," was his cool greeting. "And my lord. Shall we begin?"

Leonora sighed in vexation and explained that she was going to fetch a chaperon.

"When did you become such a stickler?" Forrester scoffed, still with that maddening, mild expression on his face. "I shall be quite able to keep you young people from getting into trouble."

"Oh, do stop it!" exclaimed Leonora, quite forgetting the presence of Lord Stone. "Didn't Major Danforth explain to you about last night? Why are you being so unlike yourself?"

"You, ma'am, are in no position to accuse me of an unexpected change. I wish you and Danforth every happiness." Forrester's lips were curved unpleasantly in a lurid imitation of his usual smile.

"What?" Leonora fell back a step, stunned.

Lord Stone rose from his chair and came forward. "I say, Forrester, the lady don't seem to like you talking so. Why don't we do the play? M'stepmother wouldn't like us to waste time."

"Did Major Danforth tell you that he and I—" Leonora spoke over the young man's diffident tones.

Forrester interrupted her. "He didn't need to. Your position was clear enough, especially after your sister warned me against disturbing you lovebirds. I left the theatre directly after having the ill fortune to interrupt you."

Well! That explained why Danforth hadn't made things right with him. Leonora frowned, trying to remember details of the past night. She hadn't asked the major if he'd completed his assigned task. She had simply assumed that he had and that Forrester hadn't wanted to come to her again because Billie was back in the box. Billie's sly air of triumph Leonora hadn't stopped to interpret, assuming that her sister was merely smug about Sir Hector's attentions.

"Sir," said Leonora, "this is one of those absurd situations I haven't experienced until now, only heard about. Don't you see, my sister said what she did to warn you off, knowing the major and I were in the box alone. I happened to be patting his hand to comfort him because he has the ill fortune to be over head and ears in love with Wilhelmina. Would you like to cry friends now, or would you rather remain vexed with me for a week or two?" She paused. "I must say it's odd to be in the middle of a coil like this. I thought misunderstandings could be avoided by honesty. And so they can. Why didn't you simply ask me last night—"

"What? And risk a scene with Danforth in the middle of a crowded theatre? Your programme of honesty is admirable, Miss Clare, but it ought to have limits."

Leonora saw, to her joy, that Forrester's eye held the familiar twinkle once again. "You may call me Leonora if you wish," she dared to say. Never had she done anything so flirtatious.

"Leonora!" said Forrester. The name sounded very sweet on his tongue. "Would you like to call me Richard?"

"Certainly, sir, in private."

"Capital. Now that we're friends again, there's something I've been longing to do. If Danforth had beaten me to it, I'd have murdered him for certain."

They were standing quite close together. It remained only for Forrester to take a step towards Leonora, draw her into his arms, and gently, ever so gently, kiss her mouth.

Leonora could not help herself. She brushed off strict principles like so many irritating insects in her happiness at his continued friendship. She melted, leaning against him.

"I say," came a squeaky voice close by.

Leonora ripped herself out of Forrester's arms. She had forgotten about Lord Stone!

"Oh, dear," was Forrester's comment. He was still looking at Leonora, eyes brimming with affection.

"Miss Clare is to become my wife," said Lord Stone, straightening his shoulders under their buckram wadding. "You can't go about kissing her."

Leonora stared. Lord Stone hadn't so much as clasped her hand, let alone asked for it.

Forrester, his lips somewhat unsteady, was bowing to Lord Stone. "My lord, forgive my boldness. You must realize that Miss Clare's beauty and charm overcame me for the merest instant and turned me into a ravening beast."

Lord Stone pursed his mouth and looked thoughtful. Leonora wondered if he would call Forrester out.

A detailed examination of the tall, broad-shouldered Forrester apparently rid that idea from the young man's mind, if it had indeed been there. "See it don't happen again. And you ain't to call her Leonora!"

Leonora rolled her eyes. The entire territorial argument was taking place without reference to her or her feelings, but she didn't like to tax Lord Stone about the matter. And she assumed Forrester didn't really mean to treat her as a nonentity; he was simply keeping her out of the unpleasantness. Surely he knew she wouldn't marry Lord Stone.

Lord Stone, his ultimatum delivered, began to pout rather like the spoilt child Leonora suspected he was. She exchanged a warning glance with Forrester. Laughing at the young man was certainly not the proper course.

Should Leonora inform Lord Stone at this moment that she had no intention of marrying him? She stood in indecision, surveying the young peer's stormy expression and tightly folded arms. No, this was not the time to make him angrier; and he probably would refuse to take her word for it in any case.

"Gentlemen, can't we forget this ever happened?" she said in her most cajoling tones. "We have work to do on the play. We must practise, Lord Stone, and I'll go and fetch my sister so that Mr. Forrester won't be, er, tempted again. And will you, my lord, swear to tell no one what you just witnessed?"

Leonora noticed that Lord Stone gazed at her with the same look of admiration he always had as he answered, "It wouldn't do to make such a mistake common knowledge, ma'am. Why, they might say he'd compromised you, and there you'd be in a real muddle."

Leonora presumed that the "muddle" would be the necessity of marrying the poor and ineligible Forrester rather than the rare catch before her. She willed herself not to laugh.

"My dear sir, you've shown a rare practicality and understanding," Forrester exclaimed, clapping the young peer on the back. "I can only be pitied, and Miss Clare must be protected. You're wise beyond your years."

"I'm turned five-and-twenty," protested the young man. "And it don't do to embarrass a lady."

"Why don't you gentlemen sit down?" Leonora suggested. She supposed it would be no use asking Lord Stone to take his leave.

Lord Stone nodded and took her advice, making a show out of finding the proper place in his manuscript. Forrester, after a last heavy-lidded glance at Leonora, did the same.

As Leonora went off to find Billie, she considered the scene which had just taken place. *Had* Forrester only been overcome by the moment? Did the kiss mean nothing to him? Leonora could not believe that; yet neither could she believe that he could have anything more serious than flirting in his mind. In any case, she had been very wrong to yield to him. Why, then, did her lapse provoke such delightful feelings in her?

Her sister, when Leonora told her about the situation, was visibly torn between joy and vexation. How delightful that Lord Stone had sought out Leonora, but how abysmally stupid of the young man to have asked Forrester to practise with them! She would be quite willing to chaperon, though it meant leaving the attentive Sir Hector.

Billie also noticed the strange, bemused expression on her sensible sister's face and asked point-blank what the trouble was. Leonora could only shrug.

How could she think up plausible excuses when she was longing with all her heart for a truly private word with Forrester—not to mention another kiss?

CHAPTER TWELVE

BILLIE COULD SENSE something new, something questionable, between her sister and Forrester. At least so it seemed to Leonora, who had to stand by and play the demure miss while Billie behaved like a snapping pug during the remainder of their time at Lady Markham's, guarding her sister from the objectionable Forrester with extraordinary zeal.

By the time the sisters reached home Leonora was seething. Worse, she was powerless to make her displeasure felt. No longer could she assure Billie that she was in no danger from Mr. Forrester, she thought as they separated to go to their respective bedrooms, Billie stopping to pick up the letters from the entryway table.

But never had she known such a mysterious gentleman, and Leonora did not like mysteries. His touch might excite her and his conversation entrance her, but one fact remained: he was a stranger. She knew less about him than she did about any one of her father's cottagers. Could she really be in love with a virtual incognito? Never in her life had she imagined herself letting go her heart to someone she did not know.

She was looking into her bedroom glass, wondering if her face could have changed from being kissed, when Billie screamed. One piercing shriek and no more, but Leonora followed it in a flash, pausing at the sitting-room hearth to pick up the poker.

Billie was standing in the open doorway of her room, letters scattered at her feet.

Leonora peeked over her sister's shoulder and drew in her breath sharply. "Papa!"

Sir John lay in Billie's bed, his white shirt open at the neck. His other clothes littered the room.

Esmé stood beside the bed, trembling. She was in her shift. As Leonora watched in fascination, Esmé addressed a flurry of Spanish to Billie.

"Papa," said Billie icily, "did I not hear you once address me as a trollop? Well, that's what *you* are. Oh, *cállate.*" The last exasperated word was presumably addressed to Esmé, whose mouth snapped shut.

Sir John coughed. For one instant Leonora thought he had the grace to look ashamed, but that expression soon passed. He took on his normal belligerent scowl and said, "Interferin' again in my affairs, is it? I've a right to my amusements."

"Papa, there can be no excuse for this." Billie's voice was as calm as though she were discussing the weather. "You are most certainly not welcome in my home as my maid's seducer."

"Humph. Between me and the chit," grumbled Sir John.

"You may be sure that there will never again be anything between you and this girl," Billie said.

"What? Ain't you going to turn her off for this? I've a mind to hire her m'self and take her back to Wiltshire."

Leonora was still unable to speak, but she wondered what Mrs. Rose would say to that.

Billie exchanged more Spanish words with Esmé while the girl scrambled into her gown and apron. Suddenly Esmé uttered a firm, "No!" She then folded her arms, and turned her back on the man in the bed.

"I've told her of your kind designs for her, Papa, and I don't think she wants to go with you," said Billie. "Whether I turn her off or not."

"What? Never heard of such ingratitude," roared Sir John. He began to get up, remembered himself, and sat back down. He turned to Esmé. "Baggage! I've given you enough gold to buy a fleet, and this is my return?"

Esmé was in the act of replacing the familiar knife in her garter, her leg propped up on the dressing table stool. She gave Sir John a malicious grin.

"My Esmé is nothing if not practical," Billie murmured in an aside to Leonora.

Leonora's eyes were still round. She had never before caught her father in the act of dalliance, though she had come uncomfortably close more than once over the years of Papa's widowhood and subsequent loss of decorum.

Billie glanced at her sister. "We'll leave Papa to dress. Esmé, would you—oh, perhaps not. Papa, you'll have to manage without a valet, but do hurry up. We'll wait for you in the sitting-room. Esmé, come with us."

The maid followed the two sisters into the other room, and, once they were seated, stood before them, the picture of regret.

Billie said, "So you met him in the street and he paid you a good sum. How dared you bring him in here? You might at least have used your own room."

Esmé rolled her eyes and said something in Spanish.

"Of course mine is a bigger bed, but I still don't excuse you. Go to your room, and we'll talk later." Billie's tone was severe, and Esmé made haste to obey, disappearing in the wink of an eye.

Leonora turned to Billie, still fighting off the shock of the situation. "What are we to do about this? Papa is right in his twisted way. You can't keep such a girl in your employ.''

''Why not?''

''Well . . .'' Leonora hesitated, caught by the note of defiance in Billie's voice. ''I don't know why not, if you can forgive her.''

''Don't worry about Esmé, dear,'' Billie said. ''She is a very good sort of girl, really. Ten to one she'll ask leave to go down to the Catholic chapel later today to confess this latest sin. A most devout creature, in her odd way.''

Leonora raised her eyebrows at this but could think of no answer to make.

''Papa will no doubt rant some more about a man's right to do as he likes,'' Billie continued. ''But there is no reason he should think of my house as his own.''

''Not to mention your maid,'' added Leonora. She could not help thinking of the situation which had driven her from home in the first place. Papa must have been mad to think a respectable daughter would stay in the house with his acknowledged lightskirt; he must be mad now to think his dalliance with Billie's servant was none of his daughters' business.

Papa and his doxies; Billie and her shameless flirting. Was Leonora the only member of the family with any sense?

An uncomfortable thought struck her. This very day she had kissed Forrester, and she wished nothing more than to repeat the experience. ''Our entire family has gone beyond the line,'' she said aloud.

Billie looked up sharply.

Sir John, rumpled and with his cravat tied askew, emerged into the room at that moment to be confronted by the cold, set faces of his progeny. ''Don't go all high and mighty with me—'' he began.

Billie held up her hand to stop his words. "You, Father, are a beast. Even if my maid invited you here, you ought to have refused. You simply must be discreet."

Sir John scowled. "You're a fine one to talk of discretion, Wilhelmina, with the things the town is saying about your habits. Throwin' yourself at every titled chap who can walk, and some who can't! Parties no female will attend! You've no room to talk. And don't worry about my place in Society. I'll have you know I've been busy about my affairs, and I've just pulled off a rare win. Last night, as a matter of fact. You may both congratulate me, for Lady Markham has agreed to make me the happiest of men."

"What is she going to do, buy you a brothel?" muttered Billie, while Leonora drew in her breath in surprise.

"Papa, you can't mean that the very day after securing Lady Markham's hand you seduced Billie's maid?"

"What an innocent you are, Leonora," said Billie, glaring at Sir John.

The baronet looked a little worried. Speaking in a voice slightly less rough than usual, he ventured, "You see, Leonora, men have needs which ladies do not. Lady Markham's a rich woman, and it suits us to join forces. But it won't mean a thing to her, mark my words, if I—"

"I don't wish to hear," Leonora said. Suddenly she was nearly in tears. "It meant something to Mama that you were after every tenant's daughter and housemaid in the county. We used to be relieved when you'd go up to Town, for then we wouldn't have to hear about what you did or try to repair the results."

"Come down off your high ropes, missy. And you, living in this nunnery of your sister's because you're too high in the instep to come home and give a sterling woman her due."

Billie made a small, infuriated sound in the back of her throat. Leonora half expected a tiny knife to appear in her sister's hands and decided to deflect comment on the insulting word "nunnery" by attacking Papa anew.

"I suppose you mean Mrs. Rose. You know what I think of her, Papa, and you know what I'll think of you if you entice poor Lady Markham into marrying you. Heavens, what if she likes you? Think how disappointed she would be."

"Oh, don't worry about that one. She can take care of herself," said Sir John with a snort.

Leonora, newly aware of the state of her own heart, didn't believe that any woman could take care of herself if her emotions were touched. Silently, she made a resolution.

Meanwhile Billie was speaking. "Papa, you must understand that I want you out of my home. And I also want your promise that you will never again come near my maid."

"You was always a thorn in my side, Wilhelmina, and you ain't changed in thirteen years. Only grown fat."

"Fat!" Billie stood and pointed to the door. "Out! Out, I say. You dreadful, disgusting, horrid . . ." She hesitated, and all vestiges of her sophisticated facade crumbled. "I hate you!" she cried out, and fled to her room in tears.

Leonora thought she could understand Billie's reaction. The insult to her figure had been the last straw. "Papa, can't you see you've hurt Billie terribly?" she said.

"She didn't hurt all of us, runnin' off with that soldier?"

"She thought she was in love." Leonora caught herself on the verge of a revealing lecture on the tender passion. She would not expose herself to her father's derision. "I'm sorry, Papa, I can't stay with you, either. Good day.'' She rose and left the room.

She leaned against her bedroom door and listened. Sir John couldn't have expected his sensible, polite younger daughter to walk out on him. He would have been surprised into a momentary silence. Would he leave? There was a rustling sound, a masculine snort, and finally the noise of the front door opening and closing.

Leonora ventured back into the empty sitting-room, dreading what she must do now. But she knew her duty when it looked her in the face.

From Billie's room drifted the sounds of sobbing, as the poor creature presumably cried out thirteen years of separation from a father whose idea of communication was the indiscriminate flinging about of insults. Leonora lifted her hand to knock, then thought better of it. She would leave a note for her sister.

She got out a sheet of paper, her ink bottle, and a fresh pen once she was back in her own room.

"Billie, I have gone to Lady Markham," was all she wrote. She left the note unsealed, propped up on the sitting room desk.

Then she put her bonnet on and walked out.

"MY DEAREST CHILD, do sit down," Lady Markham said, smiling a very wide smile as she motioned Leonora into one of the Roman chairs in her drawing-room. "You did quite well this morning in rehearsal, you know. Perhaps you've come to help dear Lord Stone with his lines? I'll be glad to chaperon."

"He and I practised earlier today. We had Mr. Forrester and my sister with us," said Leonora.

"Forrester!" Lady Markham shook her head. "That young man does disturb me. He is so familiar! But I can't think where I've seen him. I've written to Lady Prendergast, you know, to ask where her nephew is now. I'm convinced Forrester is playing a deep game. Why won't he let anyone know where he comes from?''

"I don't know."

Lady Markham shrugged. "Poor young man. And I mean that in more ways than one. You aren't letting him get too particular, are you, my dear?"

"Oh, no," said Leonora with an admirable calm. She was trusting that Lord Stone hadn't spilled the story of the kiss he had witnessed.

"Well," her ladyship said, "if you're here to talk about the play, my dear, I assure you you've nothing to worry about. You're my star performer, if you must know. Now it ain't much to be the best of a bad lot, you may say—" she noticed Leonora's dismayed look "—but you've a voice, child, and that's nothing to sneeze at. You wouldn't believe how many ladies who tread the boards would kill for a voice like yours."

"Really?" Leonora was distracted from the purpose of her call. She wondered how Lady Markham would know such a thing. "Then you must have met actresses, ma'am. At Oatlands, perhaps?" Her ladyship's bearing was so queenly that Leonora's mind leaped to the most exclusive theatrical parties she had ever head of: those the Duchess of York gave at her Kentish estate.

"No," said Lady Markham slowly, "I can't say that I've been to Oatlands, more's the pity. Now tell me, my dear: you don't have qualms about the play, do you? I'd hate to have you disappoint me so late in the game."

"Oh, I intend to go on with the play as long as your ladyship wants me," Leonora said. "I've come to see you about something else."

Lady Markham looked expectant. "My stepson?"

Leonora nearly choked. "Oh, no, ma'am. Actually, it's my...my father."

Lady Markham changed colour, fanned herself, and cleared her throat several times. "You've come to speak of Sir John?"

Leonora nodded. "Yes. Papa informed my sister and me that we are to wish you happy."

Lady Markham's shoulders relaxed visibly. "He's told you? Splendid, my dear. I haven't found a moment to break the news to dear Lord Stone or my brother-in-law. I fancy Sir Hector will think it fine, me not being called Lady Markham anymore. Some people are confused into thinking I'm his wife, and it's awkward, my owning this house instead of him. But all that's beside the point. I trust you've come to tell me you approve?"

The last words were crisp, commanding. Leonora looked into Lady Markham's face, expecting to feel contrary after being more or less told to give her blessing. To her surprise, she felt instead an element of kinship, an understanding of this woman's stiff façade. *Why, I like her!* Leonora thought in astonishment.

"My lady," she began, "I wish you every happiness. I felt compelled to come and see you to warn you—no, that's not quite the right term. To make certain you know what you are in for," she finished lamely.

"Go on," said Lady Markham.

"It's Papa. He is the sort of man who has trysts with servant girls. I don't know if it will stop on his marriage, but if I'm to take my own mother's situation as a model, I'd have to say it bodes ill."

Leonora celebrated the completion of this speech by twisting her hands in her lap. She couldn't meet Lady Markham's eye and focused instead on a firescreen near her chair.

Lady Markham's rich laugh roused her. "My dear young thing, how very sweet of you," she managed through chuckles.

Leonora swallowed. "I gather you aren't shocked?"

"Shocked? My dear, if I'm shocked at anything it's that you, a young girl, are party to your father's peccadilloes. It is a gentleman's duty to hide these little indiscretions from his nearest and dearest. Of course I know about Sir John. A woman would have to be blind not to. But he has his good qualities."

"He does?"

Leonora's incredulous expression made Lady Markham laugh again. When she had finally settled down, she wiped her wet eyes on a scrap of lace and linen and said, "My dear, you're not of an age to appreciate the subtle qualities a man like your father can bring a woman of my age. But I assure you they do exist."

"What are they?" demanded Leonora, unwilling to be fobbed off with euphemisms. Oh, heavens—surely Lady Markham wouldn't mention Papa's touted prowess in the boudoir!

"A name and title," said Lady Markham simply. "Land. And the simple fact that your Papa, unlike others of his age who are dead or married already, is a single man and living in the world. The list of eligibles dwindles when a body gets to my age. Remember that, miss. 'Gather ye rosebuds' and all of that."

"I hope you aren't marrying Papa out of any sort of desperation?" asked Leonora. She was almost afraid of the answer. She already knew that a good many marriages were matters of business. Billie, for instance, was planning to marry because she had no other choice. Yet how dismal, how sordid those sorts of bargains often were.

"Oh, I like your Papa, my girl," Lady Markham said soothingly. "I make it a rule to marry only men I like."

This seemed to call for a laugh, and Leonora managed a nervous titter. "But you're willing to tolerate his ... the terrible things he does?"

"My dear young creature, what sort of woman was your mother? Forceful at all? Did she stand up for her rights?"

Leonora had to shake her head. The very thought of her dear mama having rights was foreign to her. "She was all that was gentle and mild, the best woman in the world."

"There are other sorts of women," Lady Markham said. "I'm one. Never was called gentle in my life and don't expect to be. But you can be sure your father's doxy won't last a minute in your mother's room after we're married."

Resolutely, Leonora kept her mouth from gaping. "You know about that?"

"My dear girl, there have been rumours. Servants talk. You arrived in Cheltenham suddenly, and many people wondered why you'd left your father's house. You did the sensible thing, of course. Nobody blames you."

Leonora could only shake her head, amazed at the efficiency of gossip and not about to complain of it to a lady who she suspected led the tattlemongers.

"You have relieved my mind, Lady Markham," she said. "When Papa told us of your plans, I simply had to come and see you."

"And I'm glad you did. Now I know what a brave thing you are. You and I, Miss Clare, can whip that family of yours into shape. Lady Clare! It has a nice sound. We shall soon have your father behaving circumspectly, and we'll make that sister of yours see the error of her ways." Lady Markham paused. "No need to bristle up at me, miss, your sister *is* living on the edge, or was till you arrived in Cheltenham. But don't worry. I look forward to having another family to pull into working order. Sir Tristram Markham had no children, more's the pity.''

Leonora began to see Lady Markham's motives very clearly. By marrying Sir John she would gain two daughters to terrorize, not to mention a husband to keep in check. Why, Lord Stone must have been her ladyship's last "project." No wonder she was eager for a challenge. Papa, thought Leonora sagely, would be work enough for three managing ladies.

"Have you set a date?" she asked to change the subject. Lady Markham had not, and she welcomed the opportunity to discuss this with Leonora, who came out strongly for a Christmastide wedding and an extended trip abroad.

Leonora left the Markham house feeling oddly comforted about her father's future, Billie's, and even her own.

If only she could manage to avoid Lord Stone once she was trapped in a family relationship with the young man.

CHAPTER THIRTEEN

THE SCENE WITH PAPA and the interview with Lady Markham left Leonora exhausted. She had hardly thought of Forrester since the morning. The memory of his kiss floated somewhere in the back of her mind, not forgotten by any means but not uppermost on her list of concerns. All she wished for was leisure to think of him, but she knew she would not be granted that in the next few hours.

Billie was waiting in the sitting-room, her eyes reddened by her recent tears. She reclined upon the long chair looking as fagged as Leonora felt. "Do tell me what you were doing at Lady Markham's, Sister. Did you go to see Lord Stone? Or—" she brought out the more logical explanation "—did you leave something there this morning?"

As simply as she could, Leonora explained her errand.

Billie gasped. "You really should have asked me, Leonora, before doing any such thing. Only fancy warning Lady Markham about Papa!" She took a hard look at her sister. "What did she say?"

"That she understands Papa very well," said Leonora, preferring not to pass along her ladyship's determination to bring their family into line.

"She's a sensible woman, then, who wishes to be married even if it is to Papa. Perhaps this will make you understand *me* better," said Billie.

"I can understand wanting to marry. But Lord Carlisle? Or Sir Hector Markham? Billie, I really cannot understand wanting *that* much to be married."

"You will someday," predicted Billie with a sigh. "But I suppose there's no need to dwell upon it." She looked about her with an air of resignation and struggled to a sitting position. "Papa's latest start has left me sharp-set. Now where is that Esmé with our dinner?"

LADY MARKHAM'S ZEAL for rehearsals warred with her desire to hear the gossip of the town, and she ended by giving her players a day of leisure so that she might pay calls. The cast was to assemble to drink tea in the evening in the "playhouse," and to do a brief run-through of the more difficult sections of the comedy. Lady Markham had not been able to bear to let her slaves off entirely.

Leonora didn't want to go out to the dark little shops with Billie on this precious summer morning; nor did Billie wish to take a country walk with her. And Billie had forbidden Leonora to wander about the local lanes by herself as she used to do. The town was so full of visitors, especially strange men, that no young lady's reputation would remain unstained if she were to ramble about unattended. Billie was becoming almost ridiculously concerned with Leonora's good name lately, it being the foundation of most of her own social life.

Therefore Esmé was trailing behind Leonora when she descended into the bright summer sunshine for her walk. Both mistress and maid were carrying a basket. Moving quickly, and looking back every so often to ascertain that the solemn, sulky Esmé was still behind her, Leonora passed through the fashionable streets of the spa, where promenaders loitered and elegant sporting carriages raced by, nearly toppling the carts of the country people come in to market.

One or two young people of the fashionable set hailed her, including Portia Pickering, who was out with a younger sister and a governess. But Leonora made her greetings to all brief and businesslike, trying to give the impression that she was hurrying out upon a mission of importance. She was longing to get to the country lanes and the hills beyond.

Apparently Esmé, who emitted a theatrical sigh from time to time, was not. Leonora had hoped that the girl would cheer up once out in the bright weather.

With her only companion so taciturn as to be nearly invisible, Leonora was at leisure to think of Forrester, his kiss, and what she felt about both as the town streets became ever more rustic. Soon the walkers were passing only the occasional cottage of golden stone, and then they began the wished-for climb to Marle Hill. The slope was nothing to Leonora, but Esmé's sighs grew more frequent, her panting more pronounced. Finally Leonora consented to rest upon a fallen fence post by the roadside.

"Oh, Esmé, isn't it a lovely day?" She couldn't help talking to the girl in happiness at the beauties of nature, though she had privately settled with herself earlier that it would be best for her and Esmé to communicate as little as possible. "I mean for us to collect some foxglove today, if we can, and some gillyflowers. Do you know what the plants look like?"

Esmé gave an eloquent shrug. "Is nothing like *España.*"

"Well, of course not. Tell me, what is it like there?" Leonora felt ashamed of her previous resolution. Esmé was lonely and far from home. Leonora resolved to be friendly to the maid and to forget the disturbing episode of the day before. She would never feel comfortable with any damsel known to have sold her favours to Papa; but she might at least strive for charity. Esmé must have many good qualities, else Billie wouldn't be so fond of her.

Esmé, after a brief pause, began to give details of her native place near Segovia. She spoke no word of the war, which Leonora knew must have left its devastation. It was natural that she describe only the good memories. How far away Spain sounded, how different from England!

Leonora was gazing into the distance, and the sun was at its brightest as Esmé described the turreted castle at Segovia: "Not like these English piles of *rocas*." A tall figure was striding up the hill. A Spanish knight out of legend? No, a storybook knight would not be walking. What a very tall man this was.... Leonora smiled as she recognized Forrester.

"Miss Clare—and Esmé, is it not?" he said in greeting. "Resting from your labours?"

"We haven't laboured yet," said Leonora, casting down her eyes at the pleased look in his. "We were on our way up the hill for a view of the town, and I hope for a few blossoms." She rose, motioning Esmé to follow her example, which the maid did with a groan. "How do you happen to be here, sir?"

"I took my glass today at the Cambray Well and saw you walking by as I was on my way out of the Pump Room," he answered. "I must admit I followed you on purpose. A little slowly, to give myself time to think what I was going to say. Our interview yesterday was cut short, you know."

"I know." Leonora looked up at him, thinking of the kiss, Lord Stone's nervous blustering, and how Billie had had to be fetched at last. "My sister can be quite off-putting."

"She is only being a responsible chaperon," Forrester said with an understanding smile. "A nobody with a battered hat obviously admiring her sister? If she hadn't almost driven me from the room as she pushed you at Lord Stone, I would have told her she was remiss in her duty.''

"Oh, Mr. Forrester, I hope you're exaggerating," said Leonora. The pair started to walk on up the lane, Esmé falling into step a little distance behind.

"I thought you agreed yesterday to call me Richard." He bent his head down to hers and spoke in a low voice.

"In private, sir. In private," was Leonora's response, with a desperate glance in the direction of the maid. There was no telling how much Esmé would hear, catalogue in her memory and report back to Billie.

"As you say." Forrester gave her a wink. "I suppose the subject I was longing to open with you must be saved for some future date, since we aren't private. You wouldn't care to send the girl home? No? Well, let it stand. I had the bad luck to kiss you in front of that puppy Stone yesterday; I'd hate to initiate anything of that nature in front of your servant."

Leonora could only look at him. She was terribly afraid that her emotions could be read clearly in her eyes.

Forrester confirmed her fears. "You mustn't look at me like that, ma'am. I may be forced to kiss you again, and what would happen then?" He turned round to face Esmé. She had been plodding along, her eyes on the ground, and she almost ran into him. "Tell me, young woman, can you be bribed?"

Leonora gasped.

Esmé started, and her eyes began to gleam.

"You must not bribe this poor girl," said Leonora. "Her first loyalty is to my sister, and it is most important to me, Mr. Forrester, that she witness nothing of an improper nature."

"Oh, no, *señorita,* I keep it quiet," protested Esmé. "How much, *señor?*"

Forrester glanced at Leonora's disgruntled face, then at the obviously grasping maid. "Well, perhaps we'd better forget my idea," he said. "Here's a coin for being a good girl."

Leonora lifted up her eyes. If he only knew what method Esmé had used of gaining money the day before!

Esmé accepted the crown Forrester held out with a shrug and a small curtsy. The trio continued their walk.

Leonora felt her heart pounding. Had he wanted to offer for her today? Would he have done so if he'd been able to send Esmé away? Or was he only wishing for another kiss? Leonora knew she must be prudish and repressive if he tried such a thing again—unless the kiss were preceded by an offer of marriage.

So she was indeed thinking of marriage, then, and marriage with a man of whom she knew next to nothing. She knew that he was handsome and charming, and that he was attracted to her. Had she really reached the point of accepting such a man? Leonora was amazed at the change in herself; amazed, but strangely comfortable.

She glanced up at the tall gentleman by her side. Her hand rested within his arm, and his other hand lay on top of hers. How natural it felt to be walking along like this. And how very much she wished Esmé back in her beloved Spain!

Her pleasant dreams spun on: if Forrester did want to marry her, at last she would have the answer to his mystery. He would admit to her any shadows in his past, and tell her about his family. Leonora would forgive all irregularities and joyfully promise to follow him throughout the world.

She hesitated in her happy plans. What would they do if he were as penniless as he looked? What if he were a professional gamester or wastrel who lived by lighting on different watering places? What would a life with such a man be like? Leonora could guess. It would be scrambling in and out of lodgings as disheartening as Billie's, hoping night after night that luck would be in the cards. Nothing could be less appealing.

She let out a sigh. The truth was, there were too many unanswered questions about Mr. Forrester. One of the Clare sisters had run away with an objectionable young man; let that be enough. She looked again at her escort's handsome profile. She was so certain he was no unsavoury character. Why wouldn't he tell anyone about himself?

Suddenly she was filled with a grim determination, and she eyed him more sharply than before. He must not remain a stranger—her happiness was at stake.

Forrester saw the glance and said, "That heavy sigh indicates displeasure, ma'am, as does that unfriendly eye. What can I do to cheer you?"

"Well," Leonora said, taking a deep breath, "you might tell me a little about yourself, sir."

She felt him start. "I might return that request, ma'am. How much do I know about you?"

Leonora had a ready answer to that. "Perhaps you would like to know a few details, but you are acquainted with my family. You've met my sister and father, and you know where I come from. That's the sort of thing I mean, sir."

Forrester's eyebrows raised. "What? Because I'm a poor little orphan, I'm to be chastised?"

"There!" said Leonora. "That's something. So you're an orphan, sir. I'm so sorry. Have your parents been dead long? And have you brothers and sisters?"

"Hmm." The gentleman's smile was as bright as the summer day. "That paltry sort of thing is what satisfies you?"

"It only seems paltry. When you think about it you'll realize that you know such things about all of your acquaintance. Most people talk about themselves. Only the absence of such information makes it take on importance."

"Very well, then." Forrester's good cheer was evident as he began, "I was born in this very county, ma'am, thirty years ago. At an isolated spot in the country. I had one younger brother, who died in infancy. My mother died giving birth to him, and my father soon married again. I left home at an early age and I had the misfortune to be from home when my father was carried off by the influenza. There you have it: my very ordinary childhood, laid out for your kind approval."

"And your stepmother?" asked Leonora, more gently than she had spoken before. "Do you get along well with her?"

"Oh, marvellously well, ma'am. I doubt if she'd know me if we met in the street." He smiled mischievously. "I *know* she wouldn't know me. She hasn't seen me since I was a child of twelve."

"How sad," murmured Leonora. "Sir, I'm sorry if speaking of these things causes you pain...but I do feel that I understand you a little better."

In fact, it had occurred to Leonora that if she were a managing young lady, she might make enquiries and search for corroborating information about the Forresters. This would be Billie's tactic. Leonora, however, decided she would prefer to take everything on faith.

"This sort of talk causes me not the slightest pain," Mr. Forrester was saying. "I'm only surprised it interests you. Family affairs are often boring even to the family in question."

"Oh, no, sir. Quite the contrary."

He looked at her quizzically. "I believe you're serious. Well, fire away! Do you have more questions?"

"Do you live in the country still?" Leonora could sense that he had had enough of her queries, but she felt obliged to ask. Her fear of leading a ramshackle life, going round to watering places in search of gaming opportunities, still teased at her. How much more pleasant if Mr. Forrester should say he had a house, a humble cottage however run-down, where he and a bride might settle.

"My dear Leonora—my dear Miss Clare," said Forrester, "your curiosity is most refreshing. Not another human creature in Cheltenham has asked me where I make my home. I find that's a quality of the spa life. People who might not say how d'ye do in Town rub elbows quite freely in the more casual atmosphere of a watering place. I must hope your curiosity springs from your interest in me. And to answer you: I've been abroad for many years, off and on, and I hope to settle in my own house before long. In these lovely Cotswold Hills, in fact."

"Oh," said Leonora. This sounded promising.

They came to a sort of clearing, a field where sheep grazed and a few oaks and elms broke the view down the hill to Cheltenham. Forrester halted, turned to face Leonora and captured both her hands in his. "Now that you know all those trivial things about me, are we well enough acquainted for me to beg a dance of you at the next assembly?"

Esmé nearly crashed into them. With a Latin grumble she moved away, looking at Leonora with something like envy.

Leonora's heart thrilled at Forrester's passionate gaze. "You know you would always have a dance, sir. But Billie has decided not to attend the next assembly. So many of her admirers are beyond the dancing stage that she finds it hardly worth her while."

Forrester looked quite cast down; then his brown eyes took on a sparkle of mischief and something else. "There goes my only respectable chance to get you into my arms in the near future. I'll have to chance your maid's compliance with my black designs. I have a few coins by me."

Leonora's heart began to pound wildly as he drew her close. She was wearing a bonnet with a protective poke, and Forrester, with a grin, gently loosened its ribbons and pushed it out of the way. Then his expression changed from deviltry to a smile of the most caressing sort as his face bent down to Leonora's and his lips softly covered hers.

This time there was no Lord Stone to interrupt. Esmé was somewhere nearby, but Leonora did not worry about the maid as she felt Forrester—no, it was Richard, *her* Richard—deepen the kiss. He became insistent; his hands caressed her back and moved down to her waist. Leonora's lips parted under his, and she groaned, longing for the moment to last forever.

At last she came out of the spell. Forrester's hold loosened, and Leonora saw that the sun was still shining on the rooftops of Cheltenham and the surrounding trees. Esmé gazed determinedly at the view as she tapped her foot, arms folded.

"Oh, Richard."

"Leonora, my dearest."

"*Señorita,* there are people who come."

The imminent dive back into each other's arms was effectively cut off by these prosaic words. Leonora looked down at the hill and saw two donkey carts filled with revellers, presumably on their way to a picnic ground. And this grassy stretch would likely be their goal.

She looked shyly at Richard—or Forrester, as he must be until they could find another moment alone. He must know by now that she was in love with him. She felt dreadfully exposed, but all the same relieved to have her secret out.

"My dear girl, that was unwise," said Forrester. "But I couldn't help myself. Can you guess why?"

"No," said Leonora, though she hoped she could.

"Another time perhaps I shall tell you." He laughed as Leonora's face fell at his words. "Please understand me, my dear. I'll admit this much to you. I have family problems to sort out, things which must remain private for now, but until they are sorted out I am not quite free to do as I wish."

She stared. Family problems that would preclude—what? His offering for her, or merely telling her the whole story of his life? "Your stepmother?" she asked blankly; according to his story, he had no other close family left living.

He nodded. "Yes, she and others. There are matters I must clear up, tasks I must complete before I can honestly offer myself on a platter to any young woman. Especially one as important, as dear, as you."

Leonora's heart sang. This was nearly as good as a marriage proposal.

"The *señor* is most sensible," put in Esmé.

Leonora glared at the girl.

Esmé tossed her head, holding out her hand, palm up. She said something in rapid Spanish.

To Leonora's surprise, Forrester answered the girl in her own tongue. Some coins changed hands. Then he turned to Leonora.

"She suggests we proceed and begin to gather your, er, 'accursed plants.'"

Leonora laughed. She was slowly getting over the shock of his near proposal, and she struggled to get back a natural manner. The rest of the outing was obviously to be conducted in a more formal style than the last exciting moments. She had to agree with the wisdom of this, but all the same it was difficult not to cast herself into his arms again. "You have hidden talents, sir. Where did you learn Spanish?" she asked in a determined conversational tone.

Forrester shrugged. "The usual. A gentleman's education, a trip abroad..."

"In Spain? Not many people would choose to visit a country so terribly plagued by war."

"Spain wasn't always so distressed. Now, my dearest— Miss Clare. Shall we?"

Leonora took the offered arm and fell into step beside him again. Her basket, which she had dropped and entirely forgotten, was retrieved by Esmé.

"I think there is some foxglove nearby," murmured Leonora. The threatened picnickers were very near now; luckily they were all strangers to her.

Forrester seemed to have a slight acquaintance with one or two, but he only waved and called out brief greetings. He and the two women went on their way as the picnic party began to spread their equipment on the ground.

He was gazing on Leonora with a mixture of tenderness and desire which she could not mistake when she dared to look directly at him. But, as did she, he saw the practical reasons to maintain a tardy formality in their encounter.

Leonora did her best to keep up her end of the game, but she wondered mightily what sorts of "family problems" were plaguing him. If only she could do something to help.

She was wise enough to understand, though, that for now the subject was closed. The knowledge that his mystery involved family discretion somehow made it more understandable. She had certainly had problems enough with her own relations.

CHAPTER FOURTEEN

"THE PLAY IS COMING together splendidly, don't you think?" said Sir Hector Markham in his heartiest tones.

His nephew, who was beside him, looked miserable and did not answer.

Leonora, who happened to be standing on stage with the two gentlemen during a break in the latest rehearsal, agreed with the unexpressed sentiments of the younger.

"My lord, perhaps it won't be so bad," she ventured gently. Lord Stone looked seriously overset.

He raised his puppylike eyes to her in true dismay. "You know that ain't true, ma'am." With a limp half bow, he wandered away down the stage, the picture of hopeless dejection.

"He is so evidently reluctant to do this," Leonora said. "Perhaps her ladyship shouldn't have insisted. He may worry himself into a panic." She paused and did her best to smile at Sir Hector, never her favourite companion. "I may do the same myself," she added honestly.

"Miss Clare, you shouldn't be at all concerned. As my sister-in-law says, you are the best among us." Not being plagued by stage fright himself, Sir Hector had apparently no understanding of his nephew's plight. Now he leaned closer, and Leonora instinctively drew back. "Ah, I had been meaning to ask: might I call you Leonora? In anticipation of our coming close relationship."

The news of Sir John Clare's engagement to Lady
Markham was not yet common knowledge, but the middle-aged fiancés had informed their closest kin. Leonora's
growing pleasure in the idea of the match was offset by the
thought that she would, indeed, be connected to this awful baronet after the wedding. And so would Billie!

"I think we should retain our formality for now, Sir
Hector," she said sweetly.

She endured a few more sly comments from Sir Hector,
who could not take his leave without a hint about one
wedding in the family leading to another. When he had
gone on his way with a parting leer, Leonora sighed in relief, looking about for Forrester.

She saw him come in just as Lady Markham called the
players together and insisted on yet another run-through
of the first act. "We must hook the spectators, my dears,
not frighten them off," she bellowed briskly as Mr. Boyles
and Ensign Derwent took their places.

Leonora found an opportunity to sidle up to Forrester
in the wings and to say in a low voice, "I'm very worried
about Lord Stone, sir. Could you manage to give him a
bracing talk about how this play won't be so horrid at all?"

Forrester gave her a tender look. "Always looking out
for others, aren't you, my dear? I'd be glad to, if you think
I could help him."

"I don't know," said Leonora, "but I daresay his mama
is not the person to speak to him. She got him into it in the
first place. And I can't think of anyone else. His uncle
seems more amused than not at his plight. I—I feel so
sorry for poor Lord Stone."

"I'll try my best. You would think as much of my plight
were I in Lord Stone's shoes, wouldn't you?"

"In that case, sir, I shouldn't have to. I suspect you
could act to perfection."

He smiled in acknowledgement of her compliment. "But do realize, ma'am, that in the case of you and me, I have never been acting even for a moment."

A long look passed between them. Since their afternoon together on Marle Hill neither he nor she had alluded directly to the intimacy the encounter had produced. They had resumed their casual, friendly relations, meeting only at rehearsals, addressing each other with distant dignity. Only their eyes sometimes betrayed that a sort of understanding bound them.

So it was now. Leonora had to give herself a shake to remember that she was on the stage and that Lady Markham was imperiously demanding her presence.

"MISS CLARE, I AM COME to bid you goodbye," said Major Danforth next morning. He stood framed in Billie's doorway with his hat in his hand.

Leonora, frowning in concern, ushered him inside. "Sir, I thought you weren't going back to your regiment for another two weeks."

Danforth sighed as he accepted a chair in the sitting-room. "Well, ma'am— Where is Wilhelmina?"

"She's still dressing. She ought to appear very shortly."

"Well, ma'am—" Major Danforth leaned close to Leonora, speaking in a softened voice "—I will not stand by and see her throw herself at that Markham fellow. With your families about to be connected, there's no saying she won't get him after all. I've decided to go back early and see a bit of London life before I ship out."

"Oh, Major," said Leonora, truly stricken. "What a shame." It struck her to appeal to his masculine pride, and she added, "A little competition wouldn't stop some men."

The major wasn't biting. "I understand what you're trying to do, Miss Clare, and I'm glad you wish I could win her. But it's not a man that keeps me from Wilhelmina. I can't compete against England, or riches, nor can I offer those to her while there's the war." He paused. "Come to think of it, I don't think she'd take me in peacetime, at half pay."

Leonora said, "If it makes a difference, I'm thinking seriously of having Lady Markham intercede with Papa to get Billie's dowry settled on her. If that were to happen, the two of you could be quite comfortable."

The major shook his head.

His despondent manner annoyed Leonora, and her next words were snapped out: "Major, your business is fighting. Do you mean to surrender?"

She had just uttered the last syllables, which had the alarming effect of making Danforth's face turn brick-red, when the door to Billie's room opened, and she walked in on them.

"Danforth! How are you? Have you rung for wine, Leonora?" said Billie cheerily, sitting down by the major in a flutter of cherry-sprigged muslin: a morning gown which Leonora had insisted looked much better on Billie than on herself.

Leonora, frustrated by Danforth's hangdog look and Billie's oblivious good humour, took up the bell and rang for Esmé.

The maid soon appeared with three glasses, then proceeded to fill them from the wine decanter which stood on a table in a corner of the room.

The trio sipped wine. Leonora couldn't bear the tension emanating from Danforth. "I think the major has something to say to you, Billie. I'll be in my room." She rose, prepared to go and sew the cuffs more tightly into her Quaker costume while the major made his farewells.

"Oh, don't go, ma'am," said the major hastily, while Billie looked at Leonora in astonishment.

Billie then turned to Danforth. "Well, Major? Is something wrong?"

Leonora believed she could see decision in the major's eyes; he would declare himself before he left. She felt a greater need than ever to be out of the room, and she got up again.

"Sit down, ma'am. Please," said Danforth.

He must be taking courage from her presence. Leonora sat down, hoping that she wouldn't be too uncomfortable in the sensitive moments to come.

"What is going on here?" asked Billie in an irritated voice. She looked from one of her companions to the other and let out a gasp. "Oh—you surely aren't here to ask for Leonora's hand, Danforth? James?"

"Good Lord, no," said Danforth. "Your pardon, Miss Leonora. I owe you every respect and admire you deeply. No, Wilhelmina, you clunch, I'm here to ask for *your* blasted hand. So there!"

Billie stared for one moment, then laid a hand upon his knee. "Oh, Maj—James. Not again. You know how I feel."

"I do, and it's demmed silly," said the major, shaking off her hand. "Well, as you see, Miss Leonora, it won't serve. She'd have an orangutan if he were rich enough, but me? An honest man who loves her? Not bloody likely." He stood up, folded his arms, and turned his back.

"Major! Your language," snapped Billie.

"I was going to wait, go away and have you miss me," muttered the major in a voice barely intelligible, as his back was to the ladies. "But it won't serve. There's every chance I'll go off in the next campaign. I won't wait any longer. Goodbye, Billie."

"You never call me Billie. You say it's undignified."

The major turned to face her. "Undignified it is, and it suits a woman who'll mince about a watering place making up to any old skeleton, so long as he has a title and fat pockets."

Billie caught her breath. She got up off the sofa and said, at her fiercest, "How dare you? Get out."

"I'm going, madam, and you'll never see me again, dead or alive," was the dire reply, and Danforth pushed Billie aside and stalked towards the door.

"Billie, he's going back to his regiment today," said Leonora desperately. "You won't see him again."

Billie stared at her sister. "Don't be silly, he has a few more weeks. He told me so."

The major's hand was on the door, but he turned for one last, impassioned look at Billie. "Changed my mind. I won't stay here to see that Markham chap marry you—or worse, take you off and seduce you."

Billie's face had changed. She did emit an indignant little sound at Danforth's mention of Sir Hector, but she was looking at the major with a dazed expression. "But—James. We've never been separated before."

"High time for us to part, then, wouldn't you say," burst out Danforth. "Your servant, Miss Leonora. And goodbye, Wilhelmina." He turned from them, calmly opened the door, and disappeared.

"James!"

The name seemed torn from Billie's throat, and Leonora gaped in astonishment as Billie flew after the man. She left the front door open, and Leonora could hear perfectly the slapping sound of her slippers going down the stairs; then a distant male exclamation, followed by a series of other sounds which were easily recognizable as the accompaniments of a tender scene.

Several minutes passed, and then Billie and Major Danforth, hand in hand, appeared in the sitting-room.

"Oh, Leonora," said Billie, "I've been such a fool."

"You'll get no argument from me on that score," returned Leonora with a smile.

"And Danforth—James—and I are engaged," continued Billie. Major Danforth winked at Leonora.

"Sister!" Leonora rushed to Billie and hugged her. Then she stood on tiptoe to plant a resounding kiss on the major's rough, ruddy cheek.

Danforth had his arm around Billie's shoulders. "Well, you said it in front of a witness, m'dear. We're betrothed. Now into your bonnet and we'll be married."

"What?" cried both sisters.

The major reached into his coat pocket and came up with a paper, which he gave to Billie to read. "There it is! A licence, which I got off the bishop when we passed through London months ago. We'll go now to the parish church."

"Now?" cried Billie, staring at the licence. "How can we? And why so soon?"

"I don't trust you, my dearest life," said the major bluntly. "Let a better offer come your way and you'll wiggle out of this one."

"Never!" protested Billie.

"Humph," said the major. "Get your bonnet."

Leonora and Billie exchanged glances; likely the identical thought went through both their minds, to be voiced by Billie.

"What shall I wear?" she wailed.

Major Danforth scowled. "You'll marry me now and be done with it. That dress is fine. Good Lord, I want you to take clothes off, not put 'em on. Oh—your pardon, Miss Leonora.''

Leonora said, ''That's a lovely dress, Billie. If you put on your cherry velvet spencer and my white bonnet with the red rose, you'll look perfect.''

''But you're wearing a white dress, and I'm the bride!''

''I'll change to my lilac figured muslin. As fast as lightning, Major?''

But Danforth, seeing his dream slip away into the perilous straits of a female dressing-closet, was adamant. ''Ma'am, you look most fetching, too. A bonnet is what both of you require, for I do want you with us, Miss Leonora. Better bring Esmé, too, as a second witness. I can't have too many.''

Having rung for Esmé, Billie ran to her chamber. Leonora sped to hers to get the bonnet she had promised, donning a pretty chip-straw with white ribbons on her own account. There was some running back and forth between their rooms as Billie dithered over the shabbiness of the velvet spencer and chose one of her own bonnets in preference to Leonora's, but they were quick enough to suit even the impatient major, and ready down to the blue garter tied below Billie's knee. The tiny knife was left in her cupboard.

Esmé was waiting with Danforth in the sitting room. She had put on her plain bonnet. She was beaming.

''We go back to *España, señora?*'' she said excitedly.

''Indeed we shall. I can't be separated from my dearest James,'' said Billie ''*Verdad,* Esmé, I find England a trifle dull. Perhaps I've spent too long away at the wars. Do you know,'' and she turned to Leonora for the next words, ''even this much of Society has bored me to tears. I can't think what would have happened to me had I really married one of those other men.''

"Bored," echoed Esmé in heartfelt tones, with an eloquent shudder.

Leonora and Danforth exchanged a smile. Wellington's recent triumph at Vitoria might be as nothing in the major's mind, Leonora thought, compared to this conquest of her sister.

CHAPTER FIFTEEN

HEADS TURNED WHEN LEONORA entered Lady Markham's private theatre that evening followed by Esmé rather than Mrs. Smithers.

"I do hope your sister isn't ill?" Sir Hector said, sidling up to Leonora at the first opportunity.

"Not seriously, but she decided it wisest to remain in bed," Leonora returned, exchanging a glance with Esmé.

"A shame! Well, I hope to meet her soon, but I must say, Miss Clare, it is a delight to see you also—"

"Do excuse me, sir," Leonora interjected into the middle of Sir Hector's effusions. "I must say good evening to Lady Markham." And closely followed by Esmé, who scowled darkly at Sir Hector, she sailed off across the room.

Sir Hector, Leonora could tell from one surreptitious glance behind her, was put out for only an instant. Then he made his way in the direction of Lady Cecilia Crawe. Better that lady than oneself, Leonora thought philosophically.

Lady Markham was ensconced in her usual chair, third row centre, whence she might have the clearest view of what went on upon the stage. Leaving Esmé seated at the back next to Miss Pickering's maid, Leonora went up to make her curtsy to her hostess. A large, burly gentleman was seated close beside Lady Markham this evening. Leonora looked at the gentleman in amazement. Papa!

The secret of Billie's marriage danced inside Leonora's head as she greeted her elders. She had no leave to tell the world, but she was afraid her excitement at the Danforths' new happiness might shine through somehow.

Lady Markham made this fear a certainty when she said, "You're bursting with some news, my dear. What is it?"

"Why, nothing," answered Leonora with, she hoped, precisely the right note of surprise in her voice. "Perhaps I'm only excited about the play."

"You excited about this fustian? That won't wash," said Sir John. He looked less than pleased to have been found with his hand on Lady Markham's knee.

"You are only here to court her ladyship, Papa," retorted Leonora in a teasing tone. The middle-aged lovers looked charmingly abashed.

"Well, it's time this man saw what his daughter can do," said Lady Markham gruffly.

Leonora curtsied again, smiled impishly, and said that she had to speak to Miss Pickering about their first scene before the rehearsal began. She had just seen Portia out of the corner of her eye, saying a shy word to Richard Forrester.

The two were still standing together when Leonora approached with an eager step. Forrester had a special smile for Leonora.

"Leonora, *what* are we to do?" demanded Portia, all in a flutter. "This play is really going to come off, and I shall die of shame!"

"Why so, dear? You've learned all your lines, and even Lady Markham says your country accent is much improved."

"Because there will be quantities of people watching, that's why. My—that is, a young man I met at the assembly has been invited, and how am I to do this in front of *him?*''

"How charming! You've met someone," said Leonora warmly. She was in love; her sister was a bride; everyone in the world should be happy, too. She was beaming at Forrester, though her words were for Portia. "I trust he's someone charming?"

"Oh, yes." Portia also looked at Mr. Forrester, and Leonora understood that further particulars on the young man would be forthcoming when no gentleman was present.

"Well," continued Leonora in a bracing manner, "I'm sure the gentleman is looking forward to seeing you perform."

"Oh! Yes, he is."

"Then you can't disappoint him, my dear," put in Forrester. "Take the word of your lowly prompter. You've come on amazingly. Make sure you speak up, that's all the advice you require."

Portia dimpled and blushed. Lady Markham called to her then, barking out something about a run-through of her scene with Sir Hector. Portia directed one last, terrified look at her two friends, then hurried off.

"A stroke of luck," remarked Forrester as they were left alone. "My dearest Leonora...or should I say Miss Clare? Is this situation public or private?"

"I'm very much afraid it's public...Richard," said Leonora. "You'll notice even my father is here tonight. But I have such a piece of news! Major Danforth asked me most particularly to tell you. You see, sir, my sister and he were married today."

Forrester grinned. "What news, indeed! He told me of his hopes. So he married her today?"

"He said he didn't trust her. And he had a special licence. I'm to ask you if you'll come to a private supper at the Plough after the rehearsal, to celebrate the wedding. Esmé and I will walk from here, and if you would escort us..."

There was a pause, and Forrester, after a quick look round the room, seized Leonora's hand and kissed it. "I think you know that I'll go anywhere with you," he said in a low voice. "To our shame, Esmé probably knows it, too."

Leonora suppressed, with difficulty, the desire to reach out her arms to him. Another of those moments of awareness passed between them, stronger than any she had yet known. Though it was an odd sensation indeed for one who had no experience in matters of the heart, she seemed to be sure beyond any doubt that he did love her, was longing to declare it, and ached to hold her as much as she desired to be in his arms. She stared into his eyes, astonished by the new feelings and quite enchanted. If only he would say something... if only she would. But that was quite impossible.

By mutual accord they began a sedate promenade to the stage. It was the safest course open to them in a room so full of people.

Leonora was soon trying to lose herself in the mind and heart of Lady Amaranth. This project was most difficult when her fellow performer was one such as Lord Stone.

As the production drew nearer, Lord Stone's performance had been growing ever more erratic and ghastly. This evening was no exception.

Lady Markham appeared to have thrown up her hands and decided to let nature take its course; either that or she thought that if she ignored the matter it would go away.

Indeed, she had taken to resolutely ignoring her stepson while he performed.

"I wasn't able to set his mind at rest when I talked to him," Forrester murmured to Leonora at one point, as they watched Lord Stone make hash of a particularly clever line.

The actor Rover was a wonderful, complex character. Leonora could sense this even through Stone's dismal portrayal. Rover's lines were nearly all taken from other plays, for the character had a mania for quotations. Yet each stolen phrase expressed his own feelings perfectly. Though he played a false role during the action and indeed turned out to be someone else altogether by the play's end, and not Rover at all, he was always honest. The benevolent Quakeress Amaranth fell in love with this odd creature, and Leonora, reciting her lines and wishing she were a better performer herself, forgot about Lord Stone and thought of her love for Forrester, a man who was also playing a role of sorts. Would he turn out to be as honest, as admirable, as Jack Rover?

"You've grown some spirit, young woman," Lady Markham exclaimed in approval, when Leonora had delivered a speech in particularly animated style. "See you keep it up."

Leonora had no idea what she had been doing or how to keep it up. Accordingly, she was aware of her words and perceptibly worse during the remainder of the rehearsal. Lady Markham sighed and said nothing.

When rehearsals came to a blessed end, Leonora flatly refused her father's offer to take her home, citing Esmé as her excuse. "I can't bear to see the two of you together," she stated, "and Esmé is chaperon enough."

Sir John looked as though he wished to say something sharp, but a glance round at the crowded room seemed to alter his mood. He nodded gruffly instead and took his leave with only a good-night.

Leonora, struck by Papa's improved manners, stared after him. Perhaps Lady Markham was already having an effect on her betrothed. The Sir John of old wouldn't have hesitated to make a fuss, no matter who was listening.

In a few moments Lady Markham bustled over importantly. "Miss, I told your Papa he must see you safely back to your lodging. Did he go off and leave you? I'll give him a piece of my mind—"

"Oh, no, Lady Markham. I told Papa I didn't need him and that he must not trouble himself. I have my maid, you see."

"Humph." Lady Markham looked doubtful. "You mean you've that handsome devil, Forrester. I see him hovering across the room, his eye on you. The scamp is a talented prompter, I'll give him that, but what else is he? Take care, my girl."

"Naturally, my lady. My maid can be very fierce."

"Is that so?" Lady Markham surveyed the black-clad Esmé. "She looks it—foreign, I shouldn't wonder. Well, off you go, and get some extra practice in on the last scenes, my child. Your mind seemed to wander."

Papa and Lady Markham having been fobbed off, Leonora soon found herself safely on the way to the Plough, walking beside Forrester.

They had not gone halfway down the Royal Crescent, which gleamed ghostly white under the moon, when the sound of running feet approached behind them.

"I say!" panted Lord Stone. "Not sporting, Forrester."

"My lord, what are you doing here?" demanded Leonora. She signalled to Esmé, whose hand had clapped to her garter, not to withdraw her weapon.

"Mama said I was to see you home, but dash it all, you'd gone off with someone else." He nodded to Forrester affably indeed, considering that the other man was a rival for Leonora's affections.

"Well met, my lord," said Forrester in a thoughtful tone.

The young baron held out his arm. Now that the play rehearsals were over, he seemed to be unexpectedly light-hearted. Leonora wondered at his conceit. Maybe his title was supposed to make her drop the arm of the personable Forrester. Leonora had to concede that the actions of some women, including, up to now, her sister Billie, had probably convinced Lord Stone and many others that rank was everything to the female mind.

"Actually, sir, I wasn't going home," she said. "Mr. Forrester was escorting me to the Plough, where we are to meet my sister and a . . . a close relation."

Lord Stone's features assumed an indignant expression. "Miss Clare! I must certainly accompany you in that case. 'Tis my duty to see you safely to your destination. Seems havey-cavey to me. Going to an hotel with a man ain't at all the thing."

Leonora had to laugh. She felt Forrester shaking with suppressed chuckles at her side. "Dear sir, that's quite an understatement. But you'll notice I have my sister's maid for a chaperon." She nodded to Esmé, who was standing protectively near.

Lord Stone took one look into that person's stormy dark eyes, shivered, and turned back to Leonora. "There can be no objection to my walking along with all of you. I promised Mama."

Leonora nodded. This did sound reasonable. She exchanged a glance with the silent Forrester, received what looked like an assent, and matter-of-factly linked her other arm through Lord Stone's for the remainder of the walk.

"Dashed chivalrous of you, Stone," remarked Forrester as they went along. "The night streets of Cheltenham are no place for a lone lady; not with Race Week coming on."

No one pointed out that Leonora had already had a perfectly good escort. Indeed, Lord Stone's insistence on accompanying them seemed rather out of character. Only once before, on the occasion of Leonora's and Forrester's first kiss, had he mustered anything like as much spirit as he was showing now.

"A fine night, ain't it," Lord Stone said in a hearty tone quite unlike his usual mumbling voice, further surprising his companions.

Forrester exchanged a look with Leonora and said, "I'm happy to find you this sanguine, sir, so soon before your mother's little production. Perhaps the rehearsal tonight gave you confidence?"

"Confidence?" the young man repeated in disbelieving tones. "I? No. You were good enough to tell me the other day, sir, that I'd nothing to worry about, but dash it all, I know better."

This sounded like the Lord Stone Leonora knew. She relaxed slightly; she had begun to suspect that his chatty mood might betoken an attack of hysteria engendered by the play. She could comprehend such a feeling, but witnessing its manifestation would have been most uncomfortable.

"In fact..." Lord Stone spoke up brightly once more, looking directly at Forrester, but his words soon faded to nothing, and he ducked his head.

"My lord?" essayed Forrester, but the baron made no answer.

So went the walk down the Crescent, into the High Street, and to the Plough. Leonora became possessed of the oddest feeling that she, not Forrester, was the unwelcome third. If Stone wished to speak to Forrester, she hoped he would snatch a moment when they arrived at the Plough and then go on his way home.

Major Danforth, a beaming and relaxed Danforth, met them in the front hall of the Plough. He started at seeing Lord Stone.

"Thank you for walking with us, my lord," said Leonora in a dismissive way not many would have failed to notice.

Lord Stone, however, was not among them. "Oh, I'd be glad to stay and join your party. Your sister and a relation, I think you said?"

Danforth spoke up. "The best sort of relation: a brand new brother. Miss Leonora's sister has just made me the happiest of men, Lord Stone."

"What? But your father, Miss Clare, made no mention—"

"He doesn't yet know," explained Leonora. "They were married privately today."

"To be sure. May I come with you to toast the bride, then? A pleasure, as I'm like one of the family m'self. Lady Markham is to marry Sir John, you know. Glad to stand Mrs., er, Danforth to a bottle of champagne."

"Good Lord," muttered Forrester in a low tone Leonora barely heard. "We wouldn't want to force you to it, my dear fellow," he said more loudly, with a bow to Stone.

"Oh, no trouble at all," said the young man. "And if you could spare a moment at some point in the evening, sir? I have an idea to put to you. Need your advice, that's it. Shall we go in, Miss Clare? Which room is it, Major?"

So there it was! Stone did wish to corner Forrester, and he was prepared to go to any lengths to do it. Leonora sighed, wondering why, of all times, Lord Stone should choose this evening to sink his habitual diffidence in a sea of overfamiliarity.

Billie, dressed not in her wedding clothes, but in a low-cut gown of peacock blue, a bandeau trimmed with brilliants binding her bright curls, sat in state in the best private parlour the Plough afforded. Covers were laid for four at the sparkling centre table, and a small fire burned in the grate to take the slight chill off the summer night air. The room was cozy, lit by several branches of candles. The glow of the beeswax tapers flickered over a face so contented, so absolutely satisfied, that Leonora was almost embarrassed for her sister.

Forrester went forward at once and kissed the bride's cheek. "Mrs. Danforth, I hope you'll forgive my presence here. I don't have the good fortune to meet with your approval as a, er, friend for your sister, but I must hope you'll accept me as Danforth's good friend and your well-wisher."

Billie was completely disarmed by the speech and capitulated at once. "Mr. Forrester, though you're nearly a stranger, I must admit I've heard nothing but good of your behaviour. You're very welcome here, and I know my dear James thinks highly of you. I expect to do the same."

This was very handsome, considering what Billie's opinion of Forrester had always been, but apparently all doubts must flee in the wake of her happiness tonight. Leonora was much pleased with her sister's manners for the first time in their acquaintance with Forrester.

Lord Stone was next to approach the bride and kiss her cheek. Billie nearly fell over upon seeing he was in the room, and her reception of his kiss was a startled "What?"

Stone was instantly abashed, murmuring of his pleasure at the marriage and the liberty he was taking as a sort of brother-to-be.

"Well," said Billie, quickly recovering, "we had better ring for another place-setting. Leonora, if you would?"

Lord Stone sat down in the chair next to Billie, a shy smile on his face. Danforth and Forrester exchanged looks, and Danforth busied himself with a bottle of wine while Forrester approached Leonora.

"Does it embarrass you, my dear, to have your rival suitors face off in the same room?" he murmured into her ear.

"Really, sir." Leonora looked up with a sweet smile. A niggling sense of envy at her sister's wedding made her bolder than she would have thought possible. "Lord Stone is nothing to me. In fact, it's quite evident tonight that you are the one to whom he wishes to speak. As for you, you talk about being a suitor, but are you one?"

Forrester's answering smile was teasing and a little insolent. "I thought I'd convinced you." He captured her hand, held it briefly to his lips, and winked.

"But . . ." Leonora knew a moment of real frustration. She felt betrothed to him already, and it was maddening to have these remaining reservations as to whether he really, beyond all shadow of a doubt, meant to offer for her. If he didn't, he could talk for months of family problems which held him back, and he would know that she would wait for him. He would know, she thought with a wince, precisely because she had made her feelings clear in her response to his kisses and in a thousand honest, loving gazes into his eyes.

"My dear, you want to be sure of me," said Forrester, glancing briefly at the tableau of Billie, Lord Stone, and Danforth across the small room. Billie and Stone were conversing, and Danforth still struggled with the cork of the wine bottle. "This is hardly the place; we couldn't wish for more chaperons. Not the moment for a tender exchange."

"I don't want a tender exchange," Leonora snapped indignantly, though she wasn't sure how honest she was being. So it was true! She was transparent as glass; he knew exactly what she wanted from him. Why, then, did he not…she checked her thoughts. Of course he could do nothing; he was perfectly correct in saying that this was not the time.

Forrester's hand had somehow found itself at Leonora's back, which was turned away from the others. He caressed her spine lightly.

Leonora shivered at the touch. "Nor is this the time for touching, sir," she said with a desperate glance at the others.

"Right you are," he had time to murmur into her hair before Billie cried out sharply.

"Heavens, Leonora, how long does it take to ring a bell? Bring Mr. Forrester over here and join dear Lord Stone. He's saved a place for you right here beside us."

Leonora was forcibly reminded that her sister, though she might have seen the light in her own case, was still wishing for Leonora to marry a title, no matter what package that title came in.

Toasts to the bride started the festivities. When supper arrived, it proved to be a sumptuous affair of lobster salad, cold meats, a selection of sweet cakes and fruit, and a confectionery set-piece in the shape of a fairy castle.

"Oh, I didn't know anything half so delicate could be got in Cheltenham," said Billie in admiration of the last offering.

"Nor I," spoke up Lord Stone, and, to the surprise of all, he who had never said two sentences without looking to his stepmother for guidance, began to discourse on the theme of Confects I Have Known.

As the supper wore on it became quite evident to the assembled company that the unusually chatty Lord Stone was desperate to have a private word with Forrester. A dozen times the young man tried to persuade the others that the evening was at an end and that he and Forrester should be toddling off.

Finally Forrester took the baron up on his hints. With a regretful glance at Leonora, he said with a sigh, "Would you walk with me towards my lodging, my lord? That matter you wished to discuss . . . that private matter . . ."

Stone's pale eyes lit up in gratitude. "To be sure, sir. It ain't of much consequence, but I would be glad of a word with you."

Leonora made her farewells to both men in an odd mood of resentment. Did Lord Stone have to monopolize Richard? How she would have loved to go home in the moonlight beside the man she loved. She wondered what the baron could have to say to Forrester that was so important, and why, in heaven's name, he could not have said it at some other time.

"Odd, that," Major Danforth said when the door of the private parlour had closed upon the two men. "Ladies, should we be going, too?"

"I suppose we have not much choice," said Leonora with a sigh.

"I must give credit to Lord Stone," put in Billie. "He knows how to hint Forrester away. Most unfortunate he hasn't enough finesse to not hint himself away into the bargain."

"Oh, Billie," said Leonora. "You are still chasing moonbeams. You may count upon this one fact: I will never marry Lord Stone."

"It is a woman's prerogative to change her mind," trilled Billie. She was quite giddy from the champagne.

"Come now, m'dear," urged her bridegroom. "Ain't one wedding in the family enough? At least for the nonce."

Billie was for once easily led from her sisterly lecture when Major Danforth capped his statement with a hearty embrace.

Leonora was most grateful. She beamed at the major, feeling comfort and kinship in his understanding of her predicament. So this was what it was like to have a brother!

CHAPTER SIXTEEN

THE DRESS REHEARSAL of *Wild Oats* passed with no more dreadful occurrence than Mr. Boyles's tripping over his feet and landing with a loud crash in the middle of the stacked flats. This mishap engendered a general malaise among all the players which Lady Markham bracingly characterized as typical stage fright. A bad dress rehearsal, she assured her company, was good luck in the theatre. Leonora wondered as she often did how her ladyship knew so much about things theatrical, but she was willing to accept that she and her fellow actors could certainly do no worse than they already had.

And the rehearsal had one bright spot of a sort: Lord Stone seemed to have taken courage from his talk with Forrester on the previous night. Though the young baron's performance was uninspired, he did not show the tendency to downright agony he had been evincing of late. Leonora prayed that his stage fright had indeed passed and concentrated on her own, which was becoming quite acute.

The day of the play dawned bright, warm, and sunny despite the actors' gloom. This was also the day Sir John's horse was to run on Cleeve Downs. Leonora, being so wrapped up in her own troubles, had no desire to view the races, but she was engaged to do so. The commencement of Race Week was a festive occasion, and she had promised to make the fashionable excursion to the downs with Billie and Major Danforth.

The Danforths' married life appeared to be idyllic, and Leonora joined an affectionate and bright-eyed couple at the breakfast table. Watching them with sisterly fondness, Leonora wondered if her own romance would ever end happily. Forrester would not speak while he was burdened by what he described as family difficulties, that much she knew; but would his problem ever be solved to his satisfaction?

"Poor Leonora!" said Billie. "Are you worried about the play? Remember, my dear, by this time tomorrow you'll be out of it forever."

Leonora realized she must be looking miserable and managed a weak smile. "Perhaps I'm a bit nervous."

"The race is the very thing to take your mind off the silly theatricals," Major Danforth said with a hearty laugh. "Your father has his bad side, Miss—er, Sister Leonora, but he can pick a horse. I'm not a betting man, but I've a little something riding along with Gentleman's Fancy today."

"Now, what shall you wear?" Billie asked in a brisk manner. "Your new bonnet? There's nothing like wearing something new to put a woman in the best of spirits."

Leonora did wear her new bonnet, a pretty sage-green straw trimmed with blue ribbons and cornflowers. With it went her best summer promenade dress, a fine India muslin with cornflower sprigs sprinkled on a white background. She carried a white sunshade, for Danforth had hired an open carriage to take his ladies out to the racecourse.

Billie appeared in a carriage dress several years out of date, but so happy did she look that none but the most cattish of females would have found fault with the gown or with her pretty cottage bonnet. The new Mrs. Danforth made the loveliest picture in the world as she tripped down the shabby stairs of her lodging-house.

Leonora's mood could not but lift once they were all in the pretty landau, drawn by what Danforth called a "demmed pair of plodders." He had hired a young boy as a driver so that he might devote himself to Billie. Leonora, facing backwards, looked at the couple's entwined hands and intimate smiles all the way out of the town, up Cleeve Hill, and onto the racecourse. She could not quite deny that she would not be displeased if she, in the coming days, should find herself so happy.

Carriages by the score crowded around the track. Leonora couldn't imagine how anyone but those at the front would see the races at all. Then she noticed that several ladies as well as gentlemen were not too proud to stand up as high as possible on the seats of their carriages.

Major Danforth suggested a less athletic method of getting a better view. "What do you ladies say to taking a walk up nearer the course? We might be able to see something. Then we can come back to our picnic luncheon."

The sisters agreed, and Danforth assisted them down. He offered them each an arm and began a slow promenade in the general direction of the course; slow because the place was so crowded with other carriages, ladies and gentlemen on foot, and the various vendors and hangers-on who would be found at any outdoor festivity. Leonora noticed piemen, fruit and flower sellers, even gypsies who were reading the future, either from customers' palms or dirty packs of cards, at little makeshift tables or at the sides of gentlemen's carriages.

Leonora had been to a country fair before, and this race struck her as similar. Then, just as she had formed this thought, there was a sound of pounding hooves, and, suddenly, a great mixture of huzzas and curses.

"Are we late?" she cried.

"No," said Danforth, "Sir John's horse isn't to run till noon, and it's only eleven now. Things have started up, though."

He shepherded his ladies through the throng, pointing out the white betting post with its would-be betters, men of all classes who clamoured to put a guinea on White Cliff here, a pony on Cyprian there.

Leonora thought she recognized Papa among the crowd gathered round the post; and she was proved right when the gentlemen in question broke through the mass of men and made for the side of a tall, grey-haired lady clad in shades of puce.

"Look," Leonora whispered to her sister, "there's Lady Markham with Papa. I must go and speak with her—with them."

Billie glanced over. "You go on, dear, and if you wish to stay by her ladyship...she might have something to say to you about the play."

Leonora could take a hint: the lovers wanted to be alone. Even if it meant a tedious interlude with Papa, she supposed leaving them was the least she could do as her contribution to romance. "You two go ahead," she said. "Lady Markham may well want to talk to me."

"Leonora," spoke up Danforth, concern clear on his weather-beaten face, "be sure someone brings you back to the carriage. Can't have you lost in this mob."

Billie had the grace to look abashed for having so flippantly suggested her sister leave them. "You do know the way to the carriage, dear? There's such a crowd...."

"I shall find my way perfectly, or Lady Markham can bring me home," said Leonora with a wave of her hand.

The newlyweds walked away, and Leonora approached Lady Markham and Sir John.

The stern face of Lady Markham lit up. "Ah, Miss Clare, come out to take your mind off tonight? I'm doing the same. Your father is kind enough to share my enthusiasm for theatricals, and I can't do less than join him to see these wretched animals put through their paces."

This characterization of the day's event didn't seem to please Sir John. He scowled briefly before turning to Leonora.

"You ain't alone?" he asked in a warning tone.

"Oh, no. I was with my sister and Major Danforth, but I sent them on and said that you and Lady Markham would take care of me," Leonora responded demurely. "Wilhelmina would rather not spend too much time with you, Papa. You understand."

A blacker scowl was her reward for this mischievous impulse. "You didn't bring your maid?"

Leonora could only return an arch look to this barked query.

Lady Markham changed the subject to the utterly engrossing one of the evening's comedy. Leonora found herself being instructed, for the thousandth time, in the proper, easy way to move about on a stage.

She smiled politely and murmured the occasional word of agreement, but boredom crept up on her. She had heard the advice so often. It was still a wonder to her that Lady Markham should know so much about these matters, but she couldn't bring herself to question the lady's expertise any more than she could understand the instructions enough to make them of practical use.

Her eyes wandered, and she saw that a nearby silk marquee, erected over a table where servants were laying out cold meats, was done in her father's racing colours.

"Why, Papa," Leonora said when Lady Markham paused for breath—the control of breathing being one of the main components of her lecture, she had not paused soon—"are you hosting a party?"

"To be sure, dear girl. You and your sister and her military man are quite welcome," Lady Markham answered for Sir John. "It is merely a family party, though my dear stepson has insisted on inviting Mr. Forrester."

Leonora's eyes lit up with interest for the first time that morning.

"Yes, the girls had better come eat with us. Appearances," Sir John said with a wise look. Lady Markham nodded at him in approval and gave Leonora a knowing glance. The project of bringing the Clares into shape was evidently getting off to a fine start.

The three moved to the shade of the marquee, and the ladies situated themselves comfortably on hard chairs provided with loose cushions. Leonora saw with pleasure that the little pavilion commanded a view of the racecourse. A servant was dispatched to find Major Danforth and Billie and invite them to a picnic repast.

"And have them bring their own hamper. The more food, the better," Lady Markham directed. "Now where is that son—stepson—of mine? Sir Hector is placing a wager, but Poynton only stepped away to find Mr. Forrester."

As she uttered the words, Lord Stone arrived. He looked tolerably relaxed for a young man who was, within hours, to make a spectacle of himself before the best Society of Cheltenham. With him was a beaming Richard Forrester.

The lead actor was immediately seized upon by his mother. Lady Markham began a lecture similar to the one she had vouchsafed Leonora moments before.

"Leonora! Miss Clare," Forrester exclaimed in the meantime. "This is an unexpected delight."

Leonora smiled at him as naturally as a budding actress in her situation could do. "Sir, I'm so glad to see you. I fear I must ask you for your secret. Lord Stone no longer seems to dread the thought of the play. Could you possibly try the same words with me?"

Forrester's dark eyes twinkled. "No, ma'am, I assure you I cannot. Now don't lose courage at the last moment. I depend upon you to . . . to have an enjoyable evening."

Leonora noticed that he hadn't said, "To act with your usual style," or anything else which would not be a genuine compliment. She respected him the more for his reticence. "I doubt whether I'll manage that," she said with a brave smile, "but I can engage to try my best to perform. How very odd that I should be doing it."

"You have not much practice in playing a role other than your own, have you, dear Leonora?" asked Forrester in a low, intimate murmur.

"None at all," she said in surprise. "You know that."

"I do indeed." He looked seriously into her eyes. "I hope, my dear, that you won't hold such practice against anyone of your acquaintance. Anyone who has been playing a role, I should say."

Leonora looked at him. "You mean yourself, don't you? Are you finally—" she darted a glance about to make sure no one was paying attention and was reassured to see her father in loud conversation with a racing crony, Lady Markham still admonishing her stepson to throw his voice across the room come evening "—are you at last going to tell me what makes you such a mystery, sir?"

"I'm drawing ever nearer to the time when I may do so," he said. "There are difficulties; family members I don't wish to hurt unduly. But the tangle will be solved before long, and I want you to know now that, though I've had what I consider a proper reason, my part in this has involved deception to a degree. And you aren't fond of deception, are you, my dear?''

"No," said Leonora. She smiled. "I do understand, though, that there may be mitigating circumstances."

"Thank you," he said softly just as Billie and Major Danforth arrived, a servant carrying their hamper.

Lady Markham had perforce to let her stepson go free. He skittered to an unobtrusive spot on the other side of Sir John. Lady Markham administered gracious greetings to the major and her betrothed's elder daughter.

"Is there something the two of you would like to say to your father?" she then asked with a shrewd look.

"What's this?" said Sir John, scrutinizing the pair on his own. "Ah! A liaison, is it? Well, Daughter, you'll think twice before the next time you quiz me on my doings—"

"Sir John!" exclaimed Lady Markham.

The baronet cleared his throat and closed his jaw.

Billie straightened her plump shoulders. "This is everything that is respectable, Papa. Major Danforth and I were married recently. So there!" Eyes shining, she looked up at her new husband.

"What? Another officer?" Sir John's pale eyes seemed to start out of his head. "I never heard the like. Once wasn't enough for you, was it?"

"No," said Billie, "it was not."

Lady Markham spoke up. "Do you know, Mrs. Smithers—Mrs. Danforth—your new state becomes you." She turned to the major. "And you, Danforth, are a lucky man."

"Lucky enough," muttered Sir John, sounding abashed. To have been outdone in manners by the abrasive Lady Markham might have caused him some chagrin, Leonora thought.

The newlyweds looked suitably pleased and surprised at what was the next thing to a fatherly blessing.

"I am so glad the secret's out," exclaimed Leonora. "Thank you for your kindness, Lady Markham. I believe Billie was a little afraid to let her family know her new happiness."

"With no reason in the world," Lady Markham proclaimed. "And now let's all be comfortable and have some luncheon. With the cold chicken and strawberries you've brought, Mrs. Danforth, we'll have quite a feast."

But before the party could commence this project, interest suddenly shifted from Billie's marriage and the food to the racecourse, as familiar shouts and stampings indicated the start of another race.

"Gentleman's Fancy, go to it!" roared Sir John, pushing ahead to the best view of the horses.

Leonora, followed by Forrester and the rest of the party, gathered behind the baronet. Leonora recognized even in the line of horses the pretty little chestnut whose jockey wore the Clare silks. The company held a collective breath as the horses set off to loud acclaim.

"A stirring sight," said Forrester into Leonora's ear. He squeezed her waist under cover of the excitement, and Leonora's heart pounded for another reason than the thrill of seeing a race.

It was over almost as soon as it had begun. A rushing sound of hooves, a small, swift figure pulling ahead of the others...

"Gentleman's Fancy!" Sir John shouted. In his excitement he hugged Lady Markham tightly, dislodging the lady's headgear. She didn't appear to mind a bit.

"Good show," cried out the major.

"Oh, dear," said Leonora quietly, with a sigh.

"What is it?" Forrester asked, bending his head to hers.

She shrugged. "I brought a pound to bet on Papa's horse and forgot all about it. Now what shall I do?"

"Allow me to advise you, my dear. I can recommend Comic Muse in the next race as a most lucky choice for you."

Leonora smiled weakly in appreciation of the joke, but her mind was becoming more and more obsessed by one fact of which Forrester had unfortunately reminded her. There was no doubt about it; the hours would keep passing, and sooner or later, much sooner than she wished, she would find herself on a stage.

She was not even much encouraged when Comic Muse took second place in the next race.

CHAPTER SEVENTEEN

"I HELP YOU DRESS, *señorita,*" said Esmé, her dark eyes flashing out sympathy.

Leonora was still in her bath. She let Esmé pack up the evening dress which she would put on after the play, for Lady Markham intended to follow the performance with supper and dancing. What with the busy day at the races, Leonora was a little late.

She began to tremble as Esmé settled the stiff white collar of her Quaker dress around her shoulders. The time had really come; soon she would be standing on a stage in front of Cheltenham Society.

She pressed her hands to suddenly hot cheeks.

"'Title is vanity...'" she was muttering as she left the bedroom. Esmé followed behind with the dress and dancing slippers neatly packed in a bandbox. "'...While I entertain the rich, the hearts of the poor shall also rejoice—' Oh bother!"

"There you are," cried Major Danforth when Leonora appeared. "Why, how is this? Wilhelmina said you had been stricken with the headache, but here you are fresh as a rose."

Leonora dropped her lashes modestly. "Billie saw I was a trifle tired." She chose not to mention the bit about being sick in the basin and was glad Billie had not.

"Glad to see you're better. Nervous with the big moment upon you? Well, well, tomorrow it's all over and done with, and you can begin to enjoy yourself without anything hangin' over your head," Danforth went on.

Leonora smiled and sat down across from him, enjoying his companionship. How unfortunate that the Danforths were leaving for their regiment so soon, she thought, for she would have welcomed the chance to know the major better.

"I suppose we're waiting for Billie?" she asked.

"As the sister of the lead performer, she wants to make a good appearance," the major said with a wink. "Not that she don't look lovely in everything she wears."

Billie came out before long. She was attired in Leonora's made-over lavender dress, the one the major had once complimented her on, and a close-fitting white toque decorated with an amethyst so large Leonora knew it must be paste. A filmy white shawl was draped over Billie's plump shoulders. Both sister and husband congratulated her on her elegant appearance.

"I'm a fashionable matron, don't you know," she answered gaily. "And you, Leonora . . . well, it is a Quaker costume, after all. But you're pretty enough to look well in anything."

"I shall take that as a compliment and forget the way I look," Leonora retorted. "I expect to be worried enough about the way I sound and move about. Oh, do let's go. I so want it to be over with."

IN THE ROYAL CRESCENT pandemonium reigned in the library-turned-green-room. Lady Markham's clear voice could be heard over the chattering and shrieking as she gave last-minute directions. Quakers, country folk, "servants" ran about; but Leonora couldn't see her fellow performer, Lord Stone. Nor did she glimpse the tall figure of Richard Forrester, which must stand out in any crowd.

Leonora went up to Lady Markham, who was splendidly attired in an eye-catching grande toilette of canary satin.

"Ah, there you are, child," cried the lady. There was a feverish glint in her iron-coloured eyes tonight. Leonora thought she looked almost attractive. "At least one of my lead actors is here. And Lord Stone is with you?"

"Lord Stone? Why, no, ma'am." Leonora's eyes widened. "Is he missing?"

"I'd hoped he was with you, knowing how fond the boy is of you," Lady Markham said, looking completely distracted. "Opening night and my Rover not on the scene! Where's the understudy?"

"I—I don't believe we had one for this role," Leonora reminded her. The words "opening night" were certainly ominous. Surely Lady Markham wasn't thinking of repeating this madness? "Don't you remember, my lady, you said no one else could do justice to the part."

Lady Markham's brow darkened. "Yes, well. We shall contrive. My sweet Poynton knows how important this is to his mama—to his stepmama—and he won't fail me." She hesitated. "But should he . . . where is the butler? I'll have him read the part. Brenner!" And Lady Markham looked round the room. The butler was nowhere to be seen. Her ladyship hailed a gentleman and told him to ring the bell.

Meanwhile Portia rushed up to them, twisting the apron of her farmer's-daughter costume in her hands. "My lady!" she cried. "Leonora! The greatest tragedy!"

"Oh, Lord, what now?" murmured Lady Markham. "I assure you girls this is all of a piece with opening night jitters."

"It's one of the guests," said Portia. "My young man— that is, Mr. Clavell—just told me. Mrs. Harborough has a guest and has brought her to the play. An older lady who has come to Cheltenham to take the waters.''

"Why make a piece of work of that, child? We've plenty of chairs, and any friend of Mrs. Harborough's—"

"It's a Mrs. Siddons," said Portia.

"Mrs. Siddons!" uttered Lady Markham in the same emotional tones often employed by that legendary lady of the theatre.

The room was suddenly dead silent. "Mrs. Harborough has known her for years, and she loves the Cheltenham waters, and we are so very awful," babbled Portia into a void.

"Sarah Siddons in my house?" roared Lady Markham.

Portia hung her head and nodded.

"Good Lord, it can't be true," Lady Markham exclaimed as an excited buzz broke out again. "Come along, Miss Pickering. We'll go and look through the curtain. I know her—that is, I've seen her often enough upon the stage to know her."

Leonora was left standing alone. She felt very small in her grey and white costume. She had a feeling that the next hours would bring as much emotional turmoil as she had ever experienced in her life. Perhaps—it was a slender hope—perhaps she could bring her raw nerves and this sudden, sick feeling of imminent disaster to a fine portrayal of Lady Amaranth.

Act before Mrs. Siddons? Impossible! But perhaps Portia was wrong. More than one family in the world was named Siddons.

Lady Markham sailed back into the room at full tilt. "It's her!" she declaimed, with drama if not the strictest grammar. All the players clustered round, aghast.

"Well, it's quite an honour, upon my word," said Mr. Boyles, trying to look on the positive side. "And I'm to open! Fancy that." He turned green and rushed out of the room.

"Siddons in my audience! My Rover not here! This, ladies and gentlemen, is what true tragedy is made of," said Lady Markham, sinking down into a chair. "Well, we shall keep the spectators busy for the next little while, and Lord Stone will surely arrive." She looked round at the sea of white, scared faces. "Some of you...Ensign Derwent! I'm told you have a tolerable singing voice."

"A deuced lie, ma'am," squeaked the young officer.

"And Lady Cecilia will play for you."

"I, my lady?" gasped the young woman.

"A piece of luck I had the instrument moved in close to the stage, thinking of the dancing later," said Lady Markham. "Well! Mr. Boyles! Where is that man? Ah—" she paused as a now recovered-looking Boyles entered the room "—Mr. Boyles, go out there and announce a selection of delightful songs by Ensign Derwent, by way of prologue for our performance." She examined each member of her cast in turn. "Well? Has anyone else a hidden talent I might exploit? Where is that dratted Forrester? He looks like someone who'd sing or play."

One of the gentlemen cleared his throat. "Beg pardon, Lady Markham, but if there were any talent among us, you'd have ferreted it out by now."

"Too true," said the lady with a sigh. "Derwent? Lady Cecilia? Boyles? Out with you! Trust me, this little display will make you less nervous when it comes to the play."

"Mrs. Siddons! Doom! Disaster!" were the main currents of conversation surging through the room as the three sacrificial lambs exited through the library door to the stage. The other players soon heard applause, then a shaky pianoforte introduction, then the creditable tenor voice of Ensign Derwent.

"He'll think the Peninsula a real treat after this," murmured one of the gentlemen into Leonora's ear.

She would have laughed had she not been growing more terrified by the minute. She walked out of the room, making for the small side chamber which had been set aside for the ladies. She would sit down and try to stop trembling. *Mrs. Siddons!*

Portia followed Leonora. Holding each other by the hand for courage, they hurried to the little chamber, both smiling as they left the library to see the butler enter, very stiff and on his dignity, but clutching a copy of the play.

Lady Markham was in the ladies' sanctum already, standing before the mirror which hung over the mantelpiece. She was tucking her fine head of grey hair under a blond wig.

"Heavens, Lady Markham! What are you doing?" burst out Leonora.

The lady turned, startled. "Oh! Girls. Well, you see, this canary costume clashes so with my poor grey hair."

"But I think your hair is lovely," protested Leonora. Lady Markham's face looked oddly different under the light-coloured waves. She had lost her hawklike dignity.

"Humph. I thank you, child. But is the wig on straight?"

Portia hastened to assure her ladyship that it was. The young girl was speaking in a very soft voice Leonora hadn't heard her use since the initial rehearsals.

"Talk up when you get on stage, miss," snapped Lady Markham. She replaced her jewelled satin turban on the golden curls, poked at the headdress, and shrugged at her reflection in the glass. "Original."

"Very, my lady," responded Leonora. She supposed she could understand what this was all about. She tried to imagine being Lady Markham's age and longing for the days before grey hair. A sudden attack of nerves might well induce this odd mood. Perhaps one day Leonora would wear a blond wig too—though she rather doubted it.

"Well, I'm off to see if that miserable stepson of mine is arrived. And if worst comes to worst, the butler will do. He'll do or find himself wanting a situation." Lady Markham gave her head a final pat, reached into her reticule and came up with a pair of spectacles. She placed them on her nose, then noticed the girls eyeing her. "Never wear these; I'm too vain. But I must see everything properly tonight, don't you know. I'm too old to let vanity be my driving force. You young ladies hurry along. We can't keep the ensign warbling forever, though I quite wish we could." She bustled out of the room at her usual rapid pace.

"What do you suppose that was all about?" asked Portia, eyes round.

"I wish I knew," murmured Leonora, trying very hard to reconcile a lack of vanity with a blond wig and failing utterly. "Aren't you glad we can't sing, my dear? We might be in poor Ensign Derwent's place at this very moment."

Portia managed to return a shaky laugh to this sally.

The two fixed their hair before the mirror, murmured the lines of their scenes together, and returned to the Green Room feeling no calmer than before. They congratulated themselves, though, on not running for the front door of the house and freedom.

But had Lord Stone done so? They speculated together on this possibility as they walked on. Leonora, for one, felt that his lordship would never be seen that evening. For that matter, would he ever be seen again in Cheltenham? If he were rash enough to ruin his stepmother's pet project, he would certainly feel the sharp edge of her tongue if he dared to return.

"Can he have run off to the army?" Leonora exclaimed aloud.

Portia knew exactly to whom her friend was referring. "Oh, heavens, Leonora, do you really think..."

"I don't know what to think," said Leonora with an eloquent shrug.

CHAPTER EIGHTEEN

"I'LL DIE," Leonora said to herself. "I'll simply turn up my toes."

It was half an hour later. Leonora had no idea if Lord Stone had arrived to save the day. Lady Markham had decided to begin the play, and at this moment Mr. Boyles and Ensign Derwent were performing the opening scene.

Very shortly Mr. Hampton would enter from one side of the wings. Then, from the other side where she stood quivering now, Leonora would make her entrance as Lady Amaranth, nobly-born Quakeress.

"No," she whispered, hearing her cue.

She walked out upon the stage with friendly dignity, trying not to notice the multitudes of interested faces peering up at her from Lady Markham's chairs and sofas. It was dreadful! All those people waiting to find fault. *Mrs. Siddons!*

Leonora began to speak her lines. *Talk up!* shouted Lady Markham in her mind, and Leonora looked to the lady's chair for comfort and encouragement. To her shock, the seat was empty. Papa sat beside the thronelike spot which had been saved for the lady director, but there was no knee for him to caress.

Why would Lady Markham not be there to see her own triumph? Perhaps Lord Stone was still missing; perhaps her ladyship would be too mortified to sit by while Brenner read the part.

Leonora had little enough time to ponder this point. She and the gentlemen worked through the rest of the scene. She was proud that she didn't stutter at all, as did Mr. Boyles, nor did she run offstage, as Mr. Hampton was craven enough to do after his last line.

Hers were the last words of the first scene, and the curtain went down as she and the two remaining men exited. There was actually some applause.

She leaned against a wall, shuddering. People did this for a living! She couldn't imagine it. Would her knees ever work properly again? She hadn't fallen down, though, and her voice hadn't quavered. That was something.

She was no connoisseur of the theatre, but she had enough instinctive taste to be sure that the performers of Drury Lane and Covent Garden had nothing to worry about. And Mrs. Siddons was in the audience—no doubt having a good laugh!

Leonora ran into the Green Room, took a chair in a secluded corner, and closed her eyes. Somehow she must make ready for the scene in Act Two, her next appearance.

Her eyes flew open. Why, Scene Two of Act One was going on now! It must be, for Leonora had dimly heard the applause which had followed someone's entrance—rather loud applause, when she thought of it. Jack Rover was in Scene Two. What had happened? Was the butler indeed performing, or had Lord Stone arrived at the last moment?

Somehow Leonora believed that Lord Stone had decamped. She could well understand such a desertion, for she wished that she were several leagues away from Cheltenham herself.

The few gentlemen actors left in the Green Room acted unconcerned, and there was every indication that the play was going on as so often rehearsed. Leonora thought about going to see; perhaps she did Lord Stone a disservice in thinking he was far away. Then she shook her head. She would herself have to go back on stage soon enough.

Lady Markham hadn't planned an interval between Acts One and Two; there was merely the slight pause necessary to place the scenery of two country cottages. Leonora had heard the burst of wild applause that presumably ended Act One. Perhaps people were so grateful the play was moving along that they were willing to applaud anyone, even the butler and Mr. Hampton.

She smoothed down her costume for perhaps the hundredth time, took a deep breath and started for the wings. The cast seemed to have swelled to twice its size, and, as it was composed mainly of gentlemen, Leonora had to push past many people taller than herself in order to arrive at a convenient place in the wings. In this first scene of the second act, Farmer Gammon and his children—the daughter played by Portia Pickering—held the floor for a time; then the farmer was cruel to his poor tenant. After this came the one piece of ambitious staging the play boasted: a shower of water. Jack Rover would run in under the small sprinkling of water provided by Lady Markham's kitchen boy (who was to be sitting in the rafters with a watering can) to find shelter with the kindly tenant.

Leonora's character didn't come in until later in the scene, but she stood by in fascination, waiting to see whether it was Lord Stone or Brenner playing Rover. And where in heaven's name was Richard? He wasn't in his usual spot as prompter; a startled-looking footman stood holding the book in Forrester's accustomed place.

The curtain rose, and in walked Sir Hector Markham. A trembling Portia was also entering from the farmer's cottage which Lady Markham had designed with such attention to stagecraft.

Leonora simply couldn't watch Portia's performance, and left the wings rather than see her friend suffer. After a few moments spent in calming herself in a far corner, she went back to the stage, afraid to miss her cue. The dreadful trembling had started again as her time to enter drew near. She saw when she got there that she had missed Stone's entrance and almost immediate exit into one of the stage cottages. Sir Hector Markham was emoting with more gusto than any of the actors had so far shown. Leonora could somehow tell that he was making himself ridiculous.

She walked onstage, accompanied by the young man who played her servant, and looked into Sir Hector's eyes, which even in his role as the farmer held a roguish expression. Did the man never stop?

She found herself reciting her lines with accuracy, not anything better. Time was passing, Leonora reminded herself. This could not last forever.

Portia made her next entrance, mumbling and blushing and shaking awfully as she choked out words in her hard-won "country accent." There were a few more stiffly uttered lines from those onstage. Then all entered the farmer's stage cottage except for one unlucky actor. The audience was kind enough not to collapse in guffaws as the players fled.

The door of the cottage opened directly onto the Green Room. Leonora rushed into the sanctuary and stood against a wall. Her heart was thumping as loudly as ever it had onstage. How did people make this their profession?

Again she heard the tumultuous applause of the crowd. This convinced her that Lord Stone had not returned to take his role. But the spectators couldn't really be so thrilled by Brenner's performance, could they? He would have entered almost as the others went offstage, coming from the other pasteboard cottage. In a short while Leonora would have to go on again as well.

Mr. Boyles touched her arm, bringing her out of her reverie. "Miss Clare! You're on! You missed the cue."

"Oh, Lord." Leonora groaned, put a hand to her head, and raced through the Green Room door and then through the smaller, pasteboard cottage door. Onstage, she skidded to a stop and cried, "What tumult's this?"

The audience laughed. Leonora turned to the other actors.

If she had had the talent, or the resolve, to take to heart Lady Markham's lessons about staying in character, what she next saw might not have caused her to act as she did. She forgot that she was supposed to be Lady Amaranth, rushed up to one of the men on the stage, and exclaimed, "Richard! What are you doing here?"

As the audience hooted and shouted, some people clapping good-naturedly and, thanks to its being a private production, no one yelling obscenities or throwing fruit, Leonora said blankly, "Rover?"

"You have it," he murmured into her ear. "Lord Stone is indisposed. Remember you're the fair Quakeress." With a flourish, he swept the required bow before her and started in on his next lines.

Leonora, however, had forgotten what she was to say. Forrester whispered into her ear to prompt her, and she managed to muddle through.

Richard was a natural performer. Now Leonora knew the reason for those earlier bursts of applause at what she had believed to be Brenner's entrances. The audience was so glad to see someone perform with a tolerable flair that their enthusiasm could not be contained.

Leonora stole a look at the spectators, wanting to see how Lady Markham was taking this turn of events. Her ladyship's place was still empty. Could she be watching from another spot?

Forrester's scene with her was short, and then Leonora had some lines to go through before she was free to make her way offstage. She searched the wings, looking for Richard, and then rushed to the Green Room.

He was there, looking flushed with his triumph and more handsome than ever to Leonora's mind. She ran up to him, surrounded though he was by eager questioners, and added her mite. "What is going on? Where's Lord Stone?"

Forrester gave a general smile to the players clustered round him and answered, looking tenderly at Leonora, "The baron is unable to perform, and I know the lines. We can't disappoint Lady Markham, can we, not to mention all those people out there. Now do excuse me, all of you. The next scene is mine. Where is my waiter? Ah, there you are, Mr. Sands. Shall we go?"

He was quite correct, in his irritating way, Leonora reflected; the play must come first for now. With Forrester to help them along, perhaps this motley company could pull off a creditable performance.

They didn't do that, but so distracting was the performance of the spirited, fine-looking Jack Rover that many mumblings and awkward movements among the other cast members were forgiven.

In her scenes with Forrester, Leonora found herself fighting to remember that she was onstage. At other times, and with other actors, she felt only the remote unreality of her situation: she treading the boards, with Mrs. Siddons looking on. It couldn't be true! Did Richard know that Sarah Siddons was watching? Well, the lady would have at least one performer to approve.

Eventually Richard spoke the closing words of the comedy, and the curtain came down to spirited applause, only to be raised again as some of the happy playgoers called out for Forrester. He took a bow, signalling the rest of the cast to join him.

"Lady Markham! Madam director!" bellowed Sir John Clare. The seat beside him was still empty.

Others took up the call, and "Lady Markham!" soon rang out from all sides. Her ladyship did not appear. The calls grew louder. Leonora began to fear that something had happened to Lady Markham.

"I'll find her," she murmured to Forrester, and ran off.

She made straight for the ladies' retiring room, which she found empty. Then she enquired of a footman the way to Lady Markham's bedchamber and hurried upstairs.

"Lady Markham!" she called from outside the door. "All your guests are wishing for you to come and take a bow. I don't believe we were too awful. There was lots of applause."

Only silence answered her.

Leonora could sense that her ladyship was in there; perhaps she was shy or embarrassed. Heavens, perhaps she didn't think the performance had gone on!

"Mr. Forrester arrived to play Jack Rover," Leonora said loudly. "He was very good. They loved him."

From right inside the door came a murmur. "Is that so?"

"Oh, Lady Markham, won't you let me in? You aren't ill, are you? Papa looked very vexed that you weren't sitting by him."

There was a pause, and then the door swung open. Lady Markham was framed in it, still in her blond wig and spectacles. In addition to these dubious accessories, she now sported several patches and was quite highly rouged.

"How do I look?" she asked.

"I hardly recognize you, my lady," returned Leonora, trying to hide her shock at the lady's appearance.

Lady Markham's grey eyes were gleaming wildly behind the spectacles. "Good," she said. "I'm so many years older, Miss Clare. How would anyone know me?"

"Oh, ma'am, you mustn't talk like that," Leonora said, thinking she perceived that same feminine pride and dismay at the onset of old age which Lady Markham had betrayed earlier when she put on the wig. "Do come with me. Your guests are insisting you take your bow and receive their compliments."

Apparently Lady Markham realized that she would indeed have to face her guests sooner or later, whether or not she was satisfied with her looks. "Miss, you talk sense," she said gruffly. "Let us go. 'Twere well it were done quickly.'"

The ladies were silent as they descended the stairs. Leonora opened the dining-room door, allowed Lady Markham to pass, and then followed the lady down the centre aisle to the stage. Applause, which had quietened to a mere rattling of programmes and speculative buzzing, broke out again as people recognized Lady Markham.

"The fair director!" whooped Leonora's father as the two women ascended the steps at one side of the stage. Leonora took her place beside Forrester in the ranks of the actors, who were still giving the occasional desultory bow, and, with the exception of Forrester, looking awfully uncomfortable.

The other spectators joined Sir John in his raucous applause. "Bravo, Lady Markham! Splendid job!" cried a seasoned amateur performer and local notable, Colonel Berkeley, rising from his front-row seat.

"Encore!" cried out old Lord Carlisle.

Lady Markham bowed to all and sundry, giving gracious, dignified movements of her head in its ridiculous blond wig.

"She looks such a quiz tonight," said Portia, who had sidled up to stand by Leonora. "Which lady do you suppose is Mrs. Siddons? I was too frightened to look down before."

Leonora shrugged, scanning the audience carefully for the first time. A lady in the second row attracted her notice. A middle-aged woman dressed in the first stare of elegance, she sat almost directly ahead of the booming Sir John. Leonora's eye had lit on her at first in sympathy at her plight, seated in front of such a loud one as Papa. Now she wondered if that queenly manner, that proud head crowned with plumes, could belong to anyone but the legendary goddess of the theatre.

As Leonora pointed this lady out to Portia, the woman suddenly rose from her chair. She was directing a piercing stare onstage. Her expression changed from one of uncertainty to the happiest smile in the world.

"Bessie Barton!" she cried out in the very voice that had thrilled playgoers for over thirty years.

Lady Markham's figure swayed. In front of the awed players and all her guests she toppled over to the boards, a heap of satin and gleaming blond curls.

CHAPTER NINETEEN

THE ACTORS CROWDED ROUND the inert figure of Lady Markham as the spectators stared, fascinated, from their seats.

"Oh, my goodness," cried Leonora. "Give her air." She knelt by Lady Markham and gently patted her ladyship's rouged cheek. Was that a flicker of the eyelids? Leonora couldn't be sure. "We'd best carry her to a sofa," she decided. "Where is Papa?"

Sir John was still in his chair. The lady in front of him, who had cried out that strange name a moment before, had gathered her skirts and was moving, with an energetic tread at odds with her stately appearance, to the stage steps.

"Papa!" cried Leonora. "I need your help."

Sir John started and seemed to recover himself. He vaulted onto the stage in a remarkably lithe movement for a man of his age and habits.

"Here, Madam, what's the trouble?" he said loudly, bending down to the still figure of his betrothed.

"Really, Papa, she's unconscious," said Leonora, standing up. "Do carry her backstage to the library sofa."

Sir John balked. "By m'self?"

He did have his point. Lady Markham's Junoesque form might daunt a better man than Papa. "Sir Hector will help you," said Leonora. "Oh, Sir Hector."

The baronet, as the lady's only relation present, had to come forward from his position at the edge of the crowd.

"At your service, Miss Clare," he said with a sweeping bow, though he visibly blanched at the task ahead.

Leonora directed him about his business, and the rest of the players cleared the way as Sir Hector and Papa carried Lady Markham to the rear of the stage. Someone held aside the rear curtain, which had concealed the stage cottages, and opened the pasteboard door of the cottage which led to the library entrance. Yet another gentleman sprang to open the library door for the two puffing baronets and their unconscious lady. Some of the company followed after the strange procession.

"Did you think the comedy was over?" Forrester whispered into Leonora's ear.

Leonora shook her head, vexed at him for his lack of sympathy, and was about to enquire if anyone had sal volatile when a feathered fan tapped her on the shoulder.

She whirled round and found herself facing the majestic woman who she suspected was Mrs. Siddons.

"Young woman," said the lady, "you seem to be in charge here. I hope Bessie isn't sickly these days?"

Bessie? That name again. Well, Lady Markham's name was Elizabeth. "Oh, no, ma'am, I have never known her to faint before," Leonora answered, dropping a curtsy. "Perhaps it was the heat or the excitement."

"I'm glad to hear it," said the lady. "Ah, the years have treated her better than me, then. I'm a martyr to ill health, my dear young woman: a martyr."

Leonora nodded politely.

Many of the other spectators had followed the regal lady's lead in crowding up to the stage. Billie and Major Danforth were at the edge of the crowd. By now there was barely room to move about. Mrs. Harborough managed to push through, however, and, beaming at Leonora, said,

"I must present you to my guest, my dear. Mrs. Siddons, this is Miss Clare."

So it *was* Mrs. Siddons! Leonora's eyes were wide as she murmured her pleasure at the acquaintance.

Mrs. Siddons seemed to enjoy this awed reaction. She smiled kindly at Leonora before turning back to her hostess. "And now, my dear, I insist you present this charming Jack Rover to me." She shot an admiring look at Forrester, who stood by Leonora's side.

Mrs. Harborough fluttered her way through the courtesies. Mr. Forrester bowed over the lady's hand.

Mrs. Siddons looked at him more keenly. "Why—I never forget a face. You do look familiar, sir. Where would we have met? Could you have played in my brother's company in London as a young boy? I surely would remember...."

Forrester's eyes were sparkling with pleasure. "I was never a player before this evening, but we have met. It was in Bath, madam. I was but a boy of ten. You and my stepmother met by chance in the street...."

"Of course!" cried the lady. "Bessie's stepson! I told you at the time, young man, that that carroty hair would darken and you'd grow to break hearts. No, I never forget a face, and I can see the potential in a child at a glance."

"And I, naturally, have treasured my only encounter with the immortal Siddons," said Forrester, sweeping another, deeper bow.

Leonora stood puzzling. *"Bessie's stepson!"* But Lady Markham was Bessie. What could this mean?

"And did Bessie's little boy by Barton live?" Mrs. Siddons went on. "Poor, sickly lad. She had put him to nurse at Bath."

Forrester smiled. "I always suspected that tiny boy she took me to visit was more than a friend's child. Perhaps it was the mite's endearing way of calling my stepmother 'Mama.' Yes, madam, I have reason to believe that child is doing very well. I see him every day. He has gone into the acting profession, you know. He's been playing a part for months now.''

A sudden light dawned in Leonora's mind, and she wondered if the excitement of the performance and the thrill of meeting Mrs. Siddons had addled her brains. She didn't hesitate to interrupt Forrester's conversation with the great actress. ''Does this mean, can it possibly mean, that you are related to Lady Markham?'' she demanded, looking up into his laughing eyes.

''Lady Markham's prior marriage was to my father,'' said Forrester. ''I won't call it her first, for I suspect there was another. Not so, Mrs. Siddons?''

''I was her bridesmaid,'' the great lady of the theatre stated. ''It was in this very town, when we were doing *Venice Preserv'd*. Ah, perhaps it wasn't a wise match, but we were all young in those days, and to me it seemed wildly romantic to marry a sailor. I was newly wed myself, and you know how brides are, wanting the same thing for all their friends. 'Barton will take you off the stage,' I warned her, though, and so it proved. He wouldn't have a wife of his treading the boards. Sorry I was to hear he died all the same. A handsome devil.''

Leonora exchanged glances with her sister, for Billie was now one of those in the circle round them. What a busy life Lady Markham had led! An actress! And a first marriage to a sailor, then one to the senior Forrester, before she had presumably gone on to Lord Stone and then Sir Hector's late brother.

''In any case, good people—'' Forrester raised his voice ''—it's time for my charade to end. Lady Markham indeed married my father. A difficult task, being stepmother to an unruly child, but she managed it quite well till my unruliness extended to running away to the army. I didn't see her after that, though we exchanged friendly letters even after Father's death and her marriage to Markham.''

"Mr. Forrester," said Leonora, touching his arm, "once and for all, who was your father?''

"Haven't you guessed?'' Forrester's smile was warm, and his eyes glinted with teasing. "I'm the elder son of Thomas Manders, Baron Stone. My younger brother died in infancy.''

"But that would make you..." Leonora hesitated, afraid to voice what she thought, lest she be wrong, after all.

"Lord Stone, at your service,'' said Forrester with a bow. "Forgive me, all of you, but especially Miss Clare, for coming among you in another guise than my own. Forrester was my mother's name. And I needed some name or other, for the part of Lord Stone had already been filled.''

There was an ominous silence as Forrester paused. The only sounds to be heard were distant ones. Someone in the library called out for burnt feathers for Lady Markham, while running feet could be heard on the floor above, as servants presumably scurried about for other remedies.

Leonora kept staring at Forrester—or was it Stone? At any rate, he was Richard.

He saw her amazement, gave her a private wink, and continued. "They said I'd died in the war. So it was reported. I actually spent a goodly amount of time as a prisoner of the French. Then I escaped and made my way home to England, thinking to have a few arguments with solicitors over the disposition of my estates, which I presumed had gone to the distant cousin who was next in line for the title. Imagine my surprise when I found that the present Lord Stone was my younger brother Poynton, a baby I'd seen buried with my poor mother so many years ago." He paused. "I decided to pay a visit to Cheltenham, where Lord Stone was living, in the guise of an impecunious gentleman taking the waters, while I spied out the territory."

Leonora's eyes were even wider. The shabby clothes which contrasted so with the gentlemanly manner, the flippant talk of an unspecified illness . . . it was all beginning to make sense.

"Then who *is* Lord Stone? I mean, the young man— who is he?" demanded Mrs. Harborough, whose good-natured face bore the same confused expression as the others of Forrester's audience.

"He's Lady Markham's real son by Mr. Barton, her first husband."

Silence reigned again as the company digested this.

"What a scenario," said Mrs. Siddons with a deep, heartfelt sigh. "I can think no ill of my good friend Bessie, though. There was never a better-natured girl. Oh, do let's go see how she's getting on."

None of the eager listeners seemed reluctant to do this. With Mrs. Harborough and Mrs. Siddons in the lead, the crowd quickly emptied the stage and moved through the connecting door into the former Green Room.

Leonora and Forrester stood still as people pushed around them. When the last guest had moved on, Forrester reached out his hand.

"Well, Leonora?"

Leonora wasn't certain what he was asking, or what she ought to respond, but she addressed a new thought which had popped into her mind. "Lady Markham was an actress? And Lord Stone is really a sailor's son! Will this change Papa's plans to marry Lady Markham?"

"*That* is your major concern over this event?"

"Well, there's the matter of your behaviour, sir. Why didn't you tell me all this, Richard? Or is your name even Richard?"

"Yes, it is," the gentleman assured her. "I couldn't simply come out with such an involved tale. Lady Markham and her son had put a very convincing act together. I had to find the right moment to unmask them, or so I thought. The plot was complicated by the fact that I've always liked my stepmother. I suspect she was only being practical. She really thought I was dead, and why shouldn't she resurrect my brother if it meant that her own son could inherit a title and estates?"

"What has happened to Lord Stone? That is, I suppose he is Mr. Barton. Does he know yet of his disgrace?" Leonora couldn't help feeling sorry for the young man.

"He knows nothing yet of my true identity, if that is what you mean. My stepbrother has been sick as a dog over this play. On the night of your sister's wedding he begged me to take this role while he hid himself at the Stone estate in the country. I couldn't say no. I appreciated the joke, you know, for I knew that I would be taking his role in more than this play before long. I hope he isn't too discommoded by the truth coming out. Despite the fact that we've been jealous rivals for your affection, I've grown quite fond of the lad."

Leonora was still trying to sort out her impressions. "Major Danforth knew who you were?"

"Yes, and a dashed difficult time I've had of it trying to make him keep the secret without spilling it by accident. He's an honest sort; too honest to be good at lying."

"I should hardly consider that a flaw," said Leonora. "Did you meet the major in the army? Billie doesn't know you."

"She couldn't be acquainted with every soldier in her regiment, could she? I was sent out into the field on spying missions much of the time; and, as that was my position in the company, I didn't socialize overmuch with the officers' wives. They talk, you know. No telling when they might give a chap away. But yes, that's where I met Danforth."

Leonora was shaking her head. "This is all so very strange."

Richard smiled his most devastating smile. "Didn't I make a charming Rover?"

"Heavens, yes," said Leonora. "I might have fancied myself at the Theatre Royal. How Lady Markham would have enjoyed it if she hadn't been in hiding."

"She was hiding? Because of Mrs. Siddons, I suppose. What a pleasure it was to see that great lady after all these years! Such a pity that she's retired from the boards. Well, Leonora, what do you say? Shall we go in and see if her ladyship is recovering? She might have need of your expert care."

He held out his hand again, and this time Leonora put hers into it. They walked into the crowded library.

There the great Siddons hung over the couch of her old friend, wringing her expressive white hands as Lady Markham continued in her faint. Leonora, seeing—and smelling—that salts, burnt feathers, and various other noxious remedies had been tried already, suspected anew that Lady Markham's unconscious state was wilful.

"Let me through, please," said Leonora, with a touch of authority which had cleared her way in many a cottage sickroom. She made her way through the press of guests, touched Lady Markham on the forehead, and murmured, "My lady, everything will be all right."

The eyelids moved. Lady Markham looked into Leonora's face. "I'm lost," she whispered in a hoarse voice.

"Bessie! Oh, thank the Lord," cried Mrs. Siddons. "We have such years of talking to do, my dear. To think of finding you in such plump currant. And looking fine, I must say, though if I were you I would leave off the blond wig. Your hair was dark brown in the old days, like mine, and—"

"Sarah," muttered Lady Markham, sitting up. Her voice registered defeat as well as fatigue. "How good to see you."

Leonora reflected that Lady Markham didn't yet know the extent of her ruin; perhaps she thought that the worst was Mrs. Siddons's revelation that Lady Markham had been an actress. This would be upsetting enough to a lady well known for her prudery and prejudices.

"You must have much to talk about, ladies," Leonora said. "May I give permission for supper to be served, Lady Markham? That would clear the room."

Lady Markham managed a weak laugh. She was still looking sheepishly about the library, as if expecting the interested faces to turn grim and disapproving now that her new identity was known. "Sir Hector!" she said with a hint of her old vigour, spotting her brother-in-law.

The baronet hurried to her side.

"Tell Brenner to serve supper," directed Lady Markham. "Too weak to tell him myself."

"At once, Sister." And Sir Hector went to do her ladyship's bidding, throwing her only one amazed look. Leonora supposed that he had already heard the story of her former career and her son's masquerade.

Leonora rose from her place by Lady Markham to suggest that the various hangers-on would be more comfortable in the breakfast parlour, where the supper was to be laid. "Lady Markham needs quiet, I'm afraid," she added in her best sick-room manner.

No one could be so rude as not to allow their hostess the tranquillity so necessary to her recovery; and out they filed, some pausing to murmur of their delight at the play.

Leonora and Richard found themselves the last to go. "Well, young man? I hear you were a creditable Rover," said Lady Markham, looking up at the tall, auburn-haired gentleman.

He smiled. "And now for another touching reunion, ma'am, besides those I lately experienced when good Rover found out his true identity. Look at me carefully. Do I remind you of someone?"

Lady Markham peered through the spectacles still perched on her nose. "Yes, and so I've said many a time, young man, though my eyes ain't at all what they used to be. That dark red hair, though! Seems to throw the picture off."

"I much resemble my father, but his hair was plain brown," Richard explained to Leonora, "and I was a carroty boy with an excessive nose which I fortunately grew into. She hasn't seen me since I was twelve. Can't be blamed for not recognizing me."

"What's that you're saying, young man?" said Lady Markham.

Here Mrs. Siddons chose to step in. Walking grandly to the front of the sofa, she indicated Richard with a flourish. "This, dearest Bessie, is your stepson, little Dickon!" She paused, a gracious smile lighting her face.

Lady Markham lay back on the sofa pillows. "Dickon? Bless my soul, boy, you're supposed to be dead! Your commanding officer wrote me a very nice letter, speaking of your bravery and all of that. Was he lying?"

"Not exactly, ma'am. He was merely exaggerating." Richard bent down to kiss Lady Markham's forehead. "I look forward to renewing my acquaintance with you, Stepmama. I must warn you, though. I'm claiming my title."

Lady Markham's eyes grew bright with tears. "Of course you'll have your title back. How—how much do you know, lad?"

"I know, for I've been making my own investigations, that the young man who has been taking my part has the name of Barton."

A silence fell as Lady Markham closed her eyes again, as if in pain. Leonora could somehow sense that her ladyship was recovering her forces in some manner.

Lady Markham's eyes opened, and she smiled weakly up at Richard. "Even if my Tate were really your little brother, that's what he'd be—the younger. You shall have what's coming to you, and without any argument from me." This proclamation out, she pressed Richard's hand between her own. "I never wished you ill, my boy."

Leonora, watching this affecting scene in fascination, was at a loss to know whether Lady Markham's feelings were all sincere or stemmed at least partly from her years of Thespian training. No one could deny that her ladyship was making the most of her chance to right things with the real Lord Stone.

"I know. My lady, I admire you in a way," Richard assured his stepmother. "I'm not saying you did the right thing, but who's to say your son wouldn't have made as good a Lord Stone as my fubsy-faced second cousin, whom I haven't seen in twenty years? The temptation must have been enormous."

"You were dead," said Lady Markham flatly. "It seemed a great waste, as you say, with my poor Tate unprovided for."

"Ma'am, I wish to help him. I'll see about getting your son some gainful occupation, whatever he feels up to. We can discuss that tomorrow."

"You are a kind and generous soul," said Lady Markham with a firm nod of her head. "As was your father." More tears glittered in her ladyship's eyes. "Ah, I've had such good luck in my menfolk, with one or two small exceptions."

"One cannot help those, Bessie," put in Mrs. Siddons. "Now do let's have a good long talk about all this. So you're a titled lady now. I assure you I'm delighted. How did it all come about?"

"A long story," said Lady Markham with an embarrassed smile.

Richard glanced at Leonora. "Why don't we leave the ladies alone? They have much to talk about. And perhaps there's a corner somewhere *we* can also have a private discussion."

Leonora nodded. She made her farewells to Mrs. Siddons.

"Young lady, you have a voice," was that lady's parting statement, delivered with an approving nod. "And that is something."

Lady Markham was able to manage only a weak smile.

"And now, my lady of the voice, let's move on to the main scene of tonight's entertainment," Richard whispered into Leonora's ear as they left the room, passed through the connecting door and onto the stage.

Leonora shivered. He must mean to declare himself. It would only be a formality, of course. She had been his since he had first kissed her, weeks ago, and she suspected he knew it.

She held her breath as an awful thought struck her: what if he didn't speak? What if he wished only to say good-bye, to end their light flirtation with some practised gallantry before leaving her to her fate?

She was all trembling uneasiness as she let Richard lead her into a secluded corner of the wins.

"Oh, there you are!" cried a familiar voice, and Billie, followed by Major Danforth, rushed up to the pair. "Is it true what James just told me, sir? You are really Lord Stone, and not Forrester at all?"

"Well, yes and no, ma'am," said Richard. "I am indeed Lord Stone, but my mother's name was Forrester. If I had been born in Spain I might choose to use that name as an ordinary thing, and even here I feel I have every right."

"Oh, to be sure." Billie smiled up at him in her most charming, bedimpled manner.

"Billie," said Leonora, "if you dare to approve of this gentleman now—"

Billie ignored the sharp jab Leonora administered to the small of her back. "I have always had to admit that you are very handsome. I hope, my lord, that you don't count a sister's overprotective nature as a mark against the girl of your choice?"

"Billie!"

"Ahem! My dear," said Major Danforth. "Told you all along he was a good sort of chap, didn't I, now? No need to gush."

"And there is every need not to," Leonora exclaimed. "Billie, I thought you'd learned something about the *right* reasons to get married. You, of all people!"

"Well," said Billie, "it can't all happen at once, Sister. I am learning." Another brilliant smile was directed at the former Forrester.

The two couples were standing on one end of the stage, in full view of those who were milling about the room, supper plates in hand. Among these were Sir John and Mrs. Harborough, deep in earnest conversation. Spotting his daughters and their escorts, the baronet handed his plate to the startled lady and bounded up the steps of the stage, crying, "Say, is it true what the old cats are saying about Lady M.? That she's been running some rig on this Forrester fellow?"

"Don't think badly of her, Papa," Leonora began, reaching out a hand. "She was only trying to claim an estate for her own son when she thought Richard was dead. She's very sorry."

A delighted glint had appeared in Sir John's eyes. "What a woman! Where is she?"

Leonora glanced toward the library, while Billie stifled a laugh and the gentlemen exchanged wry looks.

"I s'pose she's with that crony of hers, the actress. So my lady was an actress, too. An actress, the next Lady Clare! That'd be a rare joke on the neighbours, what, girls?" And Sir John was off on the wings of love.

"Papa is so strange," said Leonora with a sigh.

"Perhaps it will work out. Lady Markham is a very severe woman, and Papa badly needs severity," said Billie.

"Well, speaking of severity," put in Richard, "I hate to be severe with such very good friends, but Mrs. Danforth, if you would leave us, you and the major, I must sort out a few things with your sister."

"Oh! To be sure," said Billie with a simper. She reached for Danforth's hand, and they went down the stage.

"At last!" Richard propelled Leonora into a dim corner. "My dearest, I hope you'll marry me now you know all my secrets."

Leonora stared in disbelief. "Do you call that a proper proposal?"

"You'd prefer me on one knee, begging for your hand in some moonlit garden? I might prefer that myself, but I simply couldn't wait. And, my own love, I suspect I already have you. Is that arrogant of me?"

"Very," said Leonora. "And why do you think you have me? Because you're now a rich and eligible peer?" She paused, searching his face. "How I wish you'd asked me before, when you were keeping your life a secret. Now you'll always think that your new trappings convinced me."

"Would you have accepted me as I was?" he asked. "Be honest, now."

Leonora looked into his eyes. "I don't know," she had to admit, "for I never could imagine marrying such a stranger as you were. But I certainly would have confessed my love."

Richard put a hand on her cheek. "Your love?"

"Yes," she said, determined not to dissemble. "I've loved you for the longest time."

"And I you," he said, with the happiest smile she had ever seen. "Then what do we have to discuss, my own? Trivial things. Naming the day, where to go for a bridal trip: all of that. A double wedding with Sir John and her ladyship, perhaps? No, I'd hate to wait until Christmas. What do you say to marrying soon, before your sister and the major leave for Spain?"

"That reminds me. Are you still in the army?"

"No. I sold out when I came home. I expect to have more than enough to do, what with improvements, my seat in the House, and domestic bliss. And if you're a good girl, someday I'll show the scars I already have from His Majesty's service. The army was a youthful enthusiasm, but I'm over it now."

"Scars?" Leonora looked at him in concern. "Were you really taking the waters, then, for your ailments?"

"No, my dear, merely a ruse. An excuse to be here and observe my family incognito."

"I suspected you from the first. No man as healthy as you would need to take a water cure. And another thing—"

"Leonora." Richard placed a finger upon her lips, effectively silencing her. "You still have things to learn about me. Can't we save some of them for our lifetime together? We're wasting a precious private moment on talk. One last word I must have, though: will you marry me?" He removed the finger from her lips, letting it trail down the side of her throat.

"Yes," she said. "I only wish you weren't so terribly eligible. I hate to give my sister the satisfaction."

"It is a shame. But let's risk it, my dear. Do you hesitate because you only want to kiss shabby Mr. Forrester? Perhaps the name Lord Stone is what's damping your spirits?"

"Nothing is damping my spirits but your incessant talking," Leonora said crossly. "I'm not the one chattering away. Don't you know, can't you feel that I've been longing to kiss you all the evening?"

"That's more like my honest Miss Clare," said Richard. He wrapped his arms about her, she lifted her face to his, and they were together, at last, in a perfect harmony of mind and body.

"The masks are off," murmured Richard after what seemed an eternity of searching kisses and whispered words of love.

"I never had one on. You know I am no actress," returned Leonora.

"I'm afraid all of Cheltenham knows that, my dear," were the last words she heard before she lost herself in a hearty and completely genuine embrace.

HARLEQUIN
Romance

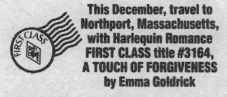

**This December, travel to
Northport, Massachusetts,
with Harlequin Romance
FIRST CLASS title #3164,
A TOUCH OF FORGIVENESS
by Emma Goldrick**

Folks in Northport called Kitty the meanest woman in town,
but she couldn't forget how they had duped her brother and
exploited her family's land. It was hard to be mean, though,
when Joel Carmody was around—his calm, good humor
made Kitty feel like a new woman. Nevertheless, a Carmody
was a Carmody, and the name meant money and power to
the townspeople.... Could Kitty really trust Joel, or was he
like all the rest?

HARLEQUIN

Romance

A Christmas tradition . . .

Imagine spending Christmas in New
Orleans with a blind stranger and his aged
guide dog—when you're supposed to be
there on your honeymoon!
#3163 Every Kind of Heaven
by Bethany Campbell

Imagine spending Christmas with a man
you once "married"—in a mock ceremony
at the age of eight!
#3166 The Forgetful Bride
by Debbie Macomber

*Available in December 1991, wherever
Harlequin books are sold.*

RXM

HARLEQUIN

Romance

is

 contemporary
and up-to-date

 heartwarming

 romantic

 exciting

 involving

 fresh and
delightful

 a short, satisfying
read

 wonderful!!

**Today's Harlequin
Romance—the traditional
choice!**

TAKE A LESSON FROM RUTH LANGAN, BRONWYN WILLIAMS, LYNDA TRENT AND MARIANNE WILLMAN...

A *history* lesson! These and many more of your favorite authors are waiting to sweep you into the world of conquistadors and countesses, pioneers and pirates. In Harlequin Historicals, you'll rediscover the romance of the past, from the Great Crusades to the days of the Gibson girls, with four exciting, sensuous stories each month.

So pick up a Harlequin Historical and travel back in time with some of the best writers in romance.... Don't let history pass you by!

HG92

HARLEQUIN
Season's Greetings

Christmas cards from relatives and friends wishing you love and happiness. Twinkling lights in the nighttime sky. Christmas—the time for magic, dreams...and possibly destiny?

Harlequin American Romance brings you SEASON'S GREETINGS. When a magical, red-cheeked, white-haired postman delivers long-lost letters, the lives of four unsuspecting couples will change forever.

Don't miss the chance to experience the magic of Christmas with these special books, coming to you from American Romance in December.

#417 UNDER THE MISTLETOE
by Rebecca Flanders
#418 CHRISTMAS IN TOYLAND
by Julie Kistler
#419 AN ANGEL IN TIME
by Stella Cameron
#420 FOR AULD LANG SYNE
by Pamela Browning

Christmas—the season when wishes *do* come true....

SG91

American Romance®